NEW YORK REVIEW BOOKS

CLASSICS

WE THINK THE WORLD OF YOU

J. R. ACKERLEY (1896–1967) was for many years the literary editor of the BBC magazine *The Listener.* His works include three memoirs, *Hindoo Holiday, My Dog Tulip,* and *My Father and Myself,* and a novel, *We Think The World of You* (all available as New York Review Books).

P. N. FURBANK is a professor emeritus at the Open University and the author of nine books, including *Diderot: A Critical Biography,* which won the Truman Capote Award for a work of literary criticism. He is a regular contributor to *The New York Review of Books* and *The Times Literary Supplement.*

WE THINK THE WORLD OF YOU

J. R. Ackerley

■

Introduction by

P. N. FURBANK

NEW YORK REVIEW BOOKS

New York

THIS IS A NEW YORK REVIEW BOOK

PUBLISHED BY THE NEW YORK REVIEW OF BOOKS

WE THINK THE WORLD OF YOU

Reprinted by arrangement with the Estate of J. R. Ackerley

First Published in Great Britain by The Bodley Head 1960

This edition published in 2000 in the United States of America by
The New York Review of Books
1755 Broadway
New York, NY 10019

Library of Congress Cataloging-in-Publication Data
Ackerley, J.R. (Joe Randoph) , 1896–1967.
   We think the world of you / by J.R. Ackerley ; introduction by
P.N. Furbank.
      p.   cm.
   ISBN 0-940322-26-9 (paperback : alk. paper)
   1. German shepherd dog Fiction. 2. Dogs—Great Britain Fiction.
I. Title.
PR6001.C4W4   2000
823'.912—dc 21   99-34916

ISBN 0-940322-26-9

Printed and bound in Great Britain by
Mackays of Chatham plc, Chatham, Kent
www.nybooks.com

To My Sister Nancy
with love and gratitude

INTRODUCTION

Advancing age has only intensified her jealousy. I have lost all my old friends, they fear her and look at me with pity or contempt. We live entirely alone. Unless with her I can never go away. I can scarcely call my soul my own. Not that I am complaining, oh no; yet sometimes as we sit and my mind wanders back to the past, to my youthful ambitions and the freedom and independence I used to enjoy, I wonder what in the world has happened to me and how it all came about. . . . But that leads me into deep waters, too deep for fathoming; it leads me into the darkness of my own mind.

THE ARRESTING AND minatory last words of *We Think the World of You* let us into the secret of this remarkable novel. Its protagonists are the narrator, an "educated" man of the professional class named Frank; Johnny, a gentle and inefficient petty criminal, who is his young working-class lover; Johnny's wife Megan; and Johnny's beautiful dog (a bitch), who eventually deserts him for Frank. We read it as a history of a set of relationships, a tale of jealousies and cross purposes; but to see it thus is, as the narrator perceives at last, an illusion. It is a story, really, only about Frank himself—about the "darkness" of his own mind and a discovery, or rather two related discoveries, to which, too late, he is brought.

Thus, though the novel has a heroine, in the shape of the dog Evie, the truth emerging from the tale is nothing about "feminine psychology." The predatory Evie is a mere stereotype of the feminine, as much so as the pantheress who takes amorous possession of a human being in Balzac's *Une Passion dans le desert*—a novel it amused Ackerley to think he was rivaling. ("She [Evie]," Ackerley wrote in a private note, "is Eve, the prototype, Shaw's tigress.") The meaning of the book lies, rather, in a discovery that Frank makes about himself—about the exorbitance and mad extravagance of his desire to be given his due, to have justice done to him.

A desire of this kind, of course, lies behind most childhood quarrels; but it takes on another aspect, growing dangerous and also farcical, when it survives into adult life. *We Think the World of You* is often wonderfully funny, and its comedy lies in Frank's dogged and irascible self-commiseration. Frank rages to himself that Johnny's wife and family, and even Evie, seem to be allowed a larger say in things than himself. Johnny is in jail for housebreaking, and of course visits to him are strictly rationed; but it seems not even to enter anyone's mind that Frank might have a claim to one. Johnny is allowed to write only so many letters, and he promises one to Frank, as "the only pal I got," but it never seems to arrive. Will no one, *no one*, Frank exclaims to himself, admit that he has rights? Thus the nemesis which overtakes him when at last someone (Evie) volunteers to grant him his rights, and more than his rights, has a frightening logic. For this first discovery leads to another, a general truth that we witness Frank perceiving in that final paragraph. It is that, in emotional matters, it may be quite fatal to get what you want.

I have said that he perceives this. It would be truer to say that he only glimpses it, so in a sense the discovery is as much the reader's as his. At any rate the suddenness with which it is sprung upon the reader is most telling.

Ackerley was rightly proud of his novel. He wrote to Stephen Spender that "it has a kind of structural perfection, like an eighteenth-century cabinet, everything

sliding nicely and full of secret drawers." The equation of
a human bitch (Megan) with a canine one (Evie)—which
is one of its "secret drawers"—is done always indirectly,
engendering hilarious cross-purpose conversations. As
Peter Parker has pointed out,[1] it is almost as a private joke
that Ackerley (or we should rather say Frank) plants a
contrast between Megan's two-piece costume and Evie's
"near sable-gray one." Equally subtle and inventive is
the way the novel is held together by variations on its
title phrase cliché, "We think the world of you." An ex-
ceedingly inadequate expression, the exasperated Frank
tells himself, typical of Johnny's whole family's refusal,
or inability, to say, or even think, anything clearly. Does
Johnny's stepfather often beat Evie, asks Frank, with a
sick feeling?

> "I wouldn't say often," replied Millie mildly.
> "...He's a kind man at heart, and he's fond of her.
> Oh yes, he thinks the world of her, he do."
> "Just like Johnny does of me!" I said, getting up.

"Well, Frank, how are you keeping?" runs Johnny's so
long-awaited and typically hopeless letter.

---

1. Peter Parker, *Ackerley: A Life of J. R. Ackerley* (Farrar, Straus & Giroux,
1989), p. 348.

"As for myself I am okay but I wish to God it was over. I shall never be able to thank . . . Megan thinks the world . . ." There was not a word about Evie. I tore it up and put it in the wastepaper basket. Whatever I might be thinking of Johnny at the moment, it was certainly *not* the world.

But eventually the phrase is given to the dog Evie, to describe her feelings about Johnny, and then it sounds right and touchingly in place. "She had perceived instantly the truth about him, that, as Millie once angrily declared, he was a gentle, tender-hearted boy, and that he thought the world of her."

How exactly Ackerley knew what he was doing with his novel is shown by some calm comments he made in the margin of a (stupid) report by a publisher's reader. "The story," he wrote, "is subtly contrived to turn completely over so that his [Frank's] 'persecutors' can be viewed in a sympathetic light." He has in mind the moment, very effective in its context, when Frank briefly comes to his senses: "Say what one might against these people, their foolish frames could not bear the iniquity I had piled upon them; they were in fact perfectly ordinary people behaving in a perfectly ordinary way."

One should not take these craftsmanlike comments of Ackerley's as spelling detachment. This novel, like *My*

Father and Myself (1968), was, as you might say, written with his heart's blood. For a writer of his talent, Ackerley's output was meager, a yawning gap of twenty-four years separating his *Hindoo Holiday* (1932) from *My Dog Tulip* (1956). His writing was always long worked over, and only done to free himself from some longstanding obsession. In *My Father and Myself* (1968) the obsession was with all the things about his life that he might so easily have told his father, had he had the wit to do so.

When I say that it does not greatly affect matters that the "she" in his novel is a dog, rather than a woman, I mean affect them artistically. As regards Ackerley personally, it hardly needs saying, his having had a long and checkered "affair" with a dog mattered vastly; and since not just one but two of his books were inspired by this affair, one is perhaps justified in saying a word about it.

In his earlier life Ackerley was, in a way, much favored by fortune. He was very good-looking, had indulgent parents and devoted friends, among them his guru E. M. Forster, and was a highly regarded literary editor. It is true that he had a complicated and harassing love life, being incorrigibly promiscuous (though he did not see it that way himself). Every three weeks or so, he would have found the love of his life. He also had a passion for telling the truth at the wrong moment. If a lover of his got into trouble—for instance for housebreaking or deserting from the army—he would picture a magnificent court-room role for himself, such as would infallibly have doubled his friend's sentence, and perhaps land himself in jail also.

"Joe," his friends would say ruefully, "would never change." They meant he had no capacity for learning from experience, and in this they may have been right. Nevertheless they were wrong in saying that he would never change. His real-life liaison with a dog (an Alsatian called Queenie) changed him radically. It turned him into a misanthrope, irascibly championing the animal king-dom against the human one.

Which is a clue for saying something else in praise of Ackerley's novel, though it may not have been part of Ackerley's conscious intention. Frank, so implacably and even hilariously determined to think the worst of Megan, is plainly a misogynist; and the novel provides a star-tlingly clear demonstration of what misogyny is. The misogynist is someone looking for a woman, someone wanting to figure magnificently in a woman's eyes and to arouse possessive feelings in her, but for whom this de-sired female conquest has to appear in a disguised shape. This represents a serious problem if the shape is mascu-line—or indeed a whole set of problems. But it would not be so, the devil whispers, if the shape were canine. Of course, in actual fact, dogs do not have gender, which is a human construction. But they have sex, upon which fantasies of gender can comfortably play. It was absolutely essential that the animal to which Frank transfers his affections from his lover Johnny should be female. There could be no writing a *We Think the World of You* about a "Towzer" or a "Rover."

—P. N. FURBANK

WE THINK
THE WORLD
OF YOU

JOHNNY WEPT WHEN I was taken down to visit him. It was a thing that I had never seen him do before. I sat down beside him on the hard bench and took his hand in mine.

"I'm so sorry, Johnny," I said.

"It couldn't be 'elped, Frank," he replied. That was characteristic anyway and, no doubt, in the circumstances, a decent thing to say; but I was in no mood to accept, even in absolution, a spineless fatalism which, repugnant in itself to my more determined nature, might also have provided an epitaph for the tomb of our friendship. But this was no moment to argue.

"What happened?" I asked. I had not gathered much from vile Megan's incoherent phone call the previous evening. He told me.

3

"If only you'd come to see me!" I said bitterly.

"I wish I 'ad now, Frank. I let you down, I know."

"I suppose I let you down too. If I'd lent you that money——"

"It wouldn't 'ave made no difference," he cut in, thrusting back the tangle of dark curly hair that had fallen over his eyes. "I needed more than that."

Yes, he was a good boy and he was exempting me, not from blame—the disturbances of the past had been none of my making—but from the very hint of it, the faintest shadow of doubt. The magnitude of the disaster suddenly overwhelmed me.

"Oh, Johnny, why didn't you confide in me? Why on earth did you keep away? I'd have given you the money if I'd known how badly you needed it. Or anything else you wanted. But you turned me down. You gave me up."

"I know you would, Frank. You've been good to me. But I didn't ought to 'ave asked you, not after the way I let you down, and I couldn't ask you no more. Besides, I didn't like to go on taking your money. I know you don't 'ave a lot. I wanted to make some of me own."

"Your own!" He had been caught house-breaking.

"Well, you know what I mean," said he, with a disarming smile. "I worked for it, didn't I?"

"And look where you are!"

"Some bastard shopped me," he said morosely. "I'd 'ave got away with it otherwise."

"Oh, Johnny, we were so happy once. Why did you let it all go? I'd have done anything for you, anything, you know that."

"It was me own fault. I was a mug. I've no one but me-self to blame." I didn't say anything. "It was the beer too," he added. I let it all pass. What was the good of going back into it now? He wanted it that way. "What d'you think I'll get?" I murmured some comfort about first offenses. "Will you do something for me now, Frank?"

But that was too much. That revolted me.

"Johnny! You're *not* going to ask me to help that disgusting woman of yours!"

"You don't want to take no notice of 'er," said he mildly.

"That's just what I'm saying," I retorted. "I *don't* want to!"

"She don't mean nothing."

"She means trouble for me and always has. If she hadn't stopped you coming to see me, all this would never have happened."

"She's jealous, that's where it is," said Johnny, blowing his nose. "She can't 'elp it."

"Johnny!" I cried again, exasperated. "The last time I saw you you called her a bloody cow!"

"Women!" he exclaimed, with a flash of the old spirit. "They're all the same!" Then he added: "But she's sorry now for what she done, I can see that. And she's been good to me since this 'appened. Ah, you can't 'elp feeling sorry for 'er."

"*I* can, easily. Is she in it too?"

"No, she ain't!" he rapped out with sudden vehemence. "She didn't know nothing about it, see? You want to be careful saying things like that!"

"Anyway I wouldn't lift a finger to help her, so don't ask me to."

"It wasn't what I was going to ask you, Frank," said Johnny in his equable way. "I was going to ask you if you could mind Evie for me till this lot's over?"

"Evie?" I was astonished. "Who on earth's Evie?"

"You know," said he reproachfully. "She's my dog. Don't you remember? I showed 'er to you last time you come."

I vaguely recollected then that, a month or more ago when, unwilling to assist him, unable to give him up, I had paid him one of those all-too-frequent visits to find out what had happened to him, what had happened to me, I had inadvertently trodden, in the darkness of his passage, on something that had squeaked and taken refuge elsewhere. If he had shown me the animal afterwards I had no memory of it. I had been in no mood to notice trivialities.

"Dear Johnny," I said smiling, "how can I possibly keep a dog?"

"She wouldn't be no trouble."

"But you know how I live. Who's to look after her?"

"She wouldn't want no looking after. Couldn't she just stay there?"

"But who's to feed her and take her out? Besides, I don't know anything about dogs, and don't want to for that matter."

"Couldn't you feed 'er when you come 'ome of an evening?"

"But I don't always come home of an evening."

"She'd be all right," said Johnny tenaciously.

"I'm awfully sorry." I tried to give the question serious thought. "Why can't Megan keep her?"

" 'Ow can she? She's got the twins and Dickie to look after. And she'll 'ave to go to work now, too."

First to be pushed out by her; now, it seemed, to be left out by him; it was insufferable!

"So have I!" I said abruptly.

"I think the world of 'er," muttered Johnny.

"Yes," I said acidly. "I noticed you'd changed your mind."

"No, Evie," said he. Anyway, Megan don't want 'er."

"Nor do I, Johnny."

He gnawed at his nails.

"I don't know what to do for the best." After a moment he added: "She's expectin'."

"But I thought she was only a puppy?"

"No, Megan."

I struck my forehead.

"What, again!" This would be the fourth. "I thought you weren't going to have any more?"

"We wasn't. But you know 'ow these things 'appen."

Then he burst into tears.

"Johnny . . . Johnny . . ." I said.

"I didn't mean to tell you, Frank," he sobbed; 'but she'll 'ave to turn out now, too. We owes some back rent. God knows what'll 'appen."

"How much?" I asked.

"About two months, I think."

"Christ! What a muddle!" I sat for a moment holding his limp hand and trying to assimilate these new disasters. Then I said: Well, Johnny, I'm sorry I can't take your dog, but I'll see you don't lose your home. And I'll go and talk to your mother. I expect we can fix things up between us. Does she know, by the way?"

"She don't yet, but she'll 'ave to. Megan's going up to tell 'er. What'll she say?"

"She loves you. You know that, or you ought to. And she's not the only one. You ought to have known that too."

He pressed my hand.

"Thanks, Frank. You're the only pal I got. I'm sorry I let you down. I won't never let you down no more. I promise you that."

The policeman who had brought me in returned.

"But whatever I do, Johnny," I said as I got up to go, "I do for *you*. I wouldn't cross the road to help that tart of yours."

I paid Johnny's back rent for him—*three* months it was—and a couple more weeks for a breather. Then I met Millie by appointment in a pub at Aldgate where we had sometimes met in the past. It was more convenient just then than going all the way to Stratford. Megan had been up to see her, Millie's letter informed me, so the bad news had already been broken.

"I'm frightfully sorry, Millie," I said, when she had spread her heavy limbs on a chair in the Saloon Bar and I had placed double gins in front of us. Not that my angry and resentful mind admitted responsibility, at any rate to her, but I knew that the fact that Johnny had set up house not far from me, in Fulham, had seemed to her an absolute guarantee of his safety.

"I don't see what it has to do with you," said she in her calm way. "I'm sure you're the best friend he ever had,

9

and if he didn't know it before, he knows it now, poor boy. If I blamed anyone I'd blame her. She's his wife and should have looked after him better."

"He says she didn't know."

"Of course he does," said Millie stoutly. "My Johnny always took the blame for everything, ever since he was little and got into trouble at school. He wouldn't never let the other boys suffer, even if they'd been bigger scamps than him; he always took it all on himself. I'm not saying she *did* know, but I'd like to see a 'usband of mine get up to them tricks without *me* knowing!" she added, laying an emphatic hand on a knee that was twice the breadth of my own.

Millie had been married four times. She had been my char when I had a flat in Holborn, until the war came and blew me out of it and I migrated to the other side of London, to the riverside at Barnes. But we had kept in touch since and I had often visited her in Stratford, where she lived. An exceptionally strong bond united us, we were both bewitched by her son; but before that young man's flashing figure appeared upon the scene, at first in the guise of a butcher's boy, to reduce me to the same almost servile condition to which he had long ago reduced her, I had liked her for herself, for her forth-rightness and good nature, the fat jollity of her rather childish mind, and the unswerving honesty of her moral code—a quality which, I think we had both guessed before the present catastrophe proved it, she had not passed on to Johnny. His cheerful and impudent lack of it, indeed, had seemed part of his charm.

"But I don't blame no one," she concluded. "What he done wasn't right, there's no getting away from that, and I'm sorry he done it. Tom and me would have helped him if he'd asked."

He had asked me and I had refused. She would never have refused, I knew. She would have put up with anything from him, anything. . . . But then her love for him was different from mine, less demanding. I had refused, but that lay between him and me.

"So would I. I helped him a lot, as you know, until that woman of his stopped him coming to see me. He hasn't been near me these last two months. She even intercepted my letters to him."

"You don't like her, Frank, do you?" said Millie, fixing her large blue gaze upon me. She knew my opinion perfectly well, and shared it; but whenever we met we indulged our personal rancors by taking Megan apart, and this was one of her favorite opening gambits.

"I love her."

"That's not what you used to say about her," said she severely.

"No, dear. I was only moderating my language."

11

"I don't understand you when you use them long words."

"I'm sorry, Millie. I think she's hell. Will that do?"

"I never liked her meself," said Millie judiciously, "and never pretended otherwise. I was sorry he picked up with her in the first place, as I told him. Tom never liked her neither, he says you can't trust the Welsh. But she's Johnny's wife and I haven't got nothing against her, she's always kept her place with me, so I wouldn't like to say nothing."

"Nor would I!" I remarked grimly.

Millie shot me another look.

"I never know how to take you," she said with a laugh.

"Why on earth did he marry her?" I continued bitterly. "I warned him not to and he always said he wasn't such a mug. Everything was perfectly all right when he was just living with her and the twins in Chatham, and coming up to stay with me or you as he pleased. He belonged to us all then. But as soon as Dickie was on the way she got working on him, and he was too weak to stand up to her. I knew she'd start interfering if she got a legal grip on him, and so she did. Her true character was instantly revealed, and now he can't call his soul his own."

"Of course I don't know nothing about all that," said Millie placidly.

"I've told you often enough!" I snapped—and though

12

the Fates must have been chuckling, the echoes of their mirth were not to reach me for some years.

"Well, what's done's done, and you saw more of them than I did. Shall we have another drink? It's my turn." Millie always paid her shot. I took her money and brought them. "What d'you think he'll get?" she asked when I was seated.

"He won't get off, I'm afraid."

"Tom didn't think so neither." We sat for a moment in silence. "They want me to take Dickie so as she can go to work."

"Are you going to?"

"I'd like to, but I don't see how I can, not without giving up my job, and I can't afford to do that."

"Can't Ida lend a hand?" Ida was her married daughter, Johnny's sister.

"She lives too far off to be always popping in."

"Well, couldn't you put him in one of those day nurseries?"

"We haven't got one near us. I could get someone to mind him, but it would cost."

"I'll help you if you like." Why on earth did I say it? They would have muddled through somehow, no doubt, and it was nothing to do with me, all this. Looking at me straight, Millie seemed to think the same.

"Why should you? You've done enough already,

paying the rent for her, or so she told me. Why did you do that, seeing what you think of her?"

"Dear Millie, I didn't do it for *her*! I wouldn't do a thing for her, except wring her neck! I did it for *him*, worthless though he is."

"Now don't you go speaking against him!" said she sharply. "He'd never say nothing but nice about you."

"I'm sorry, Millie. I didn't mean it. I love him, as you know."

"That's better," said she comfortably.

"What about the twins?" I asked. "What's to become of them?"

"Oh, I'm not taking the three of them!" cried Millie going off into one of her gusts of laughter. "Megan reckons she can manage Rita, and she's sending Gwen over to her mother's in Cardiff."

"There's to be a fourth, I understand."

"Yes, she told me, and sorry I was to hear it. She don't seem able to keep the three of them decent as it is."

"Well, you'd like Dickie?"

"Oo yes. I think the world of him. So does Tom."

Personally I thought the child both plain and stupid, but there's no accounting for tastes.

"Well then that's settled. How much do you think he'll cost? Would thirty bob a week cover it?"

"I could manage on that," said Millie promptly. Then

she added: "But you must come up and see him some-times. I wouldn't take the help otherwise."

"Yes, of course. I'll bring the money up each month. How's that?"

"That'll be nice," said Millie cheerfully. "I haven't seen much of you since Johnny left us." This was a home truth, and I began to excuse myself, but "Not that I blame you for that," she added, in that calm, sympathetic way of hers which seemed always to convey a true perception of my feeling for her son.

Determined as I was to do as little as possible for, to have as little as possible to do with, Johnny's wife, it became increasingly plain in the days that followed that not merely was she not to be avoided, but that I would have to be associated with her far more than I had ever been in the past. For the circumstances, which she was quick to seize and turn to the advantage of enhancing her own im-portance, constituted her the main, indeed the only, link between Johnny and the outside world. To me, at any rate, already too accustomed to her vigilant form planted obstructively between us, it was excessively galling to have to accept it now in the same position though in a dif-ferent guise. Usually idle and inert when she was not scratching Johnny's face or hurling the crockery about in

one of her jealous furies, she became as busy as a tele-
graph boy, dashing from place to place; and though she
knew better than to direct towards Barnes the social energy with which she flew between Johnny and Millie, she
was often on the phone. But she was smart. That Welsh
voice which, I well knew, was capable of raising the roof,
was now toneless and impassive, almost secretarial in its
formality. From her I learnt that Johnny had been com-
mitted for trial to Quarter Sessions, that he was at
Brixton, that he wanted to see me.

"When?" I asked.

"You can go any time," said the dull voice. "I go almost every day."

"What day are you *not* going?"

There was a pause the other end.

"I shan't be going Thursday."

"Very well. Tell him I'll see him then."

It was a more composed, almost, at first sight, the old
gay, carefree Johnny who confronted me behind the glass
panel in the visitor's booth; but I soon sensed that the
glittering eye and cheerful swagger were caused by the
nervous excitement in which he was living. His mind
was wholly preoccupied with the question of his im-
pending fate, and his charming boyish face was flushed
and eager. He talked a great deal, on a rather shrill note,
of what the other denizens of the jail, wider boys than

himself, thought of his chances, using the prison slang he had already picked up. The general opinion appeared to be that though the "beaks" were inclined to be " 'ot" on what he'd done, he wouldn't get more than six months. That, with remission for good conduct, came to only four.

"I could do that on me 'ead," said he.

It seemed that he could have a "mouthpiece"—a poor prisoner's defense counsel—but there was a nominal fee of three guineas. I said I would pay it. Also he was "doing his nut" for some "snout." I said I would provide cigarettes.

"Megan's sorry for what she done, Frank," he said, fixing upon me his beautiful luminous gaze. 'She says she won't never open your letters no more or stop me coming to see you. And I've told 'er I'm going away with you for your 'olidays when this lot's over." (This was an invitation I had often pressed upon him and which his wife had always defeated). "She don't mind. She thinks the world of you now."

Possibly I was getting a little tired of that phrase. In this context it seemed too much. I made a rude noise.

"Will you go and see 'er for me, Frank, when I'm inside?"

The pane of glass sundered us, as we had been sundered by her these many lonely weeks. Out of reach still, behind it he stood, his clear, brown eyes gazing into mine. The collar of his shirt was open, and the tendons of his honey-colored neck were visible where it joined the shoulders. This warm color was not sunburn but the natural tint of his flesh; the whole of his smooth, unblemished torso to the flat stomach and narrow waist glowed with it as though bathed in perpetual sunlight. The word "Yes" rose to my lips, but——

"I'm sorry, Johnny," I said.

"It don't matter. I know 'ow you feel. I'll be writing you."

"I'll be waiting for it, Johnny. And I'll come and visit you whenever you ask me—so long as you don't ask me with Megan!"

Soon afterwards he came up for trial and, in spite of his three-guinea mouthpiece, was sent to prison for a year.

The long bus ride down the Mile End Road to Stratford seemed interminable. It was Boxing Day, for Millie had written to say that although I would be welcome on Christmas Day itself, they had felt that Johnny would expect them to ask Megan then, and so perhaps I would prefer to come on one of the other days. "Not that I shall have the heart to do much, Johnny being where he is. This is the first Christmas at home he ever missed." It was a mild, moist afternoon and, as the bus trundled along through the ugly, stricken landscape I thought sadly of the vanished days when, with the figure of Johnny standing at the end of it, this had seemed to me the most exciting journey in the world. Ah well, I could at any rate talk to Millie about him, and she always gave one a warm welcome.

Warm indeed! I had forgotten the fug of the Winders' winter kitchen. Millie and Tom were both in it, and baby Dickie enthroned on a high chair which Ida had kindly lent. He was being fed with bread and jam at a table which, in spite of Millie's lack of heart, was lavishly spread with good things. I gave her a kiss, clasped Tom's horny hand, and turned to my "nephew," as it seemed Dickie had now become, since I was referred to as his uncle. In view of the fact that he was Johnny's son and heir I had always been well-disposed towards him and had gone out of my way to cultivate his good opinion; but for some reason, perhaps because I am not used to children and may not know the best way of approach, my overtures had never met with conspicuous success. As soon as I bent over him he burst into tears.

"Dear me!" I said. "That's not very polite!"

"Now, Dickie," said Millie, clucking round, "what will uncle think of you if you go pulling faces like that?"

"What indeed! I shan't give him the present I've brought him!" And I nervously pressed a golliwog into the child's sticky hand. He cast it to the floor with a howl.

" 'E don't seem to like you," said Tom, with the cheerful self-satisfaction of those who consider themselves in a strong position.

"He's not himself yet," said Millie kindly. "Oh, Frank, you should have seen him when he come! He *was* in a state, poor kid! His little bottom and legs was all red and sore where he'd been laying in his own water! "Just look at that!" I says to Tom when I comes to unpin him. "Fancy letting him go like that!" But I never did think her much of a mother, whatever she may be as a wife. Of course she has her troubles, I know that, but it don't excuse her for neglecting baby. She *must* be a lazy girl. . . ."

There was a good deal more of this; Millie was obviously enjoying being a mother again. When the theme seemed exhausted, I turned to Tom.

"Well, Tom, how are you? It's some time since I saw you."

"Mustn't grumble," said he in his chewing way. "I've a bit of a cold in me 'ead."

Small wonder, I thought, considering the stifling atmosphere in which they lived. But I only said:

"I'm sure it couldn't be in your feet!" He was wearing a pair of bright red carpet slippers. "Are they a Christmas present?"

"Ah-h, the wife give 'em me."

"We can see him coming now, can't we?" said Millie, with one of her cackles. "Do you like them, Frank?"

"Like them! I want them!" How thoughtlessly do we tempt providence! Little did I suppose that, to some extent at any rate, the preposterous objects would eventually be mine. . . .

Poor old Tom!—if one thought of him at all, one thought of him like that, and not merely because he suffered from piles. Bleak, scraggy, taciturn, and considerably Millie's senior, he was no more than a background figure to her warm, expansive personality, and one came to accept him kindlily as such, as part of the furniture of her life. It is idle, as I have already observed, to speculate about human relationships, but she herself once seemed to think he needed explanation and told me that his courtship of her had begun when she was quite a girl and persisted through all her previous marriages, becoming articulate again in the interregnums. Fourth time lucky, for she had taken him in the end. Such plodding constancy might have made him a romantic figure, but he was only a dreary one, and had for me not even the reflected glory of being Johnny's father. Moreover, the inexorability he had shown in his courtship was also, if one was not careful, revealed in his speech. Generally a silent, ruminative sort of man, he was liable, if addressed, to respond, and would launch, in his slow, monotonous, complacent way, into reminiscences, usually concerned with the First World War, which seemed to have neither direction, end, nor point, excepting always to exhibit himself, in a climax one had learnt to foresee but which Millie seldom allowed him to reach, as having come off best. Poor old Tom! Though Millie constantly brought him in in her friendly way, it was the kind of bringing in that firmly left him out, for she either did not wait for replies to the questions she put to him or answered them herself. One came to follow her example in this humane and self-protective treatment, and to accord him always a hearty but perfunctory friendliness which invited him out of his silence, only to thrust him as rapidly as possible back into it again.

It was a pleasant visit (pleasanter for me when I had asked whether we might have the window open a little and been conceded a tiny crack), though subdued: the shadow of Johnny naturally lay somberly upon us all. While we were talking about him, the scullery door was pushed open and a dog came in.

"Hullo, Evie," said Millie.

I had forgotten all about Johnny's dog.

"So this is the creature he wanted me to take?"

"Yes, he couldn't get no one to mind her, so I had to have her in the end. Not that I wanted her, the scamp."

She was certainly a pretty bitch, a few months old,

rather large and long-legged, and lavishly affectionate in that fawning, insinuating way puppies have.

"I've just been worming 'er," said Tom, who had resumed his habitual arm-chair by the fire.

"Oh," I said politely. "Did she have worms?"

"All puppies 'as worms. They're born with 'em."

Evie had now clambered on to my lap and was smothering my face with licks.

"Dickie should take a lesson in greetings from this," I said laughing and trying to protect my mouth.

"P'raps she thinks you're Johnny."

Dear Millie! She often made remarks like this which thrilled me to such an extent that they had upon me almost a physical effect. To be identified with Johnny!

"Do you know what's good for worms?" asked Tom.

"No," I said repressively.

" 'Uman 'air chopped up in treacle. My old grand-dad told me that. There wasn't much 'e didn't know about dogs. . . ."

"Now leave him alone, do!" Millie exclaimed to Evie. "Or I'll have to put you out!'

" 'Ere, Evie!" called Tom, and she scrambled up on to his knees and began to lick his gray, cadaverous face. "Tobaccer's good, too. I 'ad a dog once what ate up all the fag-ends in the street. If they was burning 'e'd stub 'em out first with 'is paw. 'E kept 'isself free from worms. . . ."

"Have you still got that picture of Johnny?" I asked Millie, wiping from my lips the moisture of the dog's tongue. I had suddenly remembered it, an enlarged photograph of him that hung over the mantelpiece in the front room. Millie laughed:

"Why, did you think I'd throw it away?"

"Can I go and look at it?"

"Of course you can." She was pleased. "You always liked that picture, didn't you?"

Indeed yes, I had always liked it and almost a year had passed since I had last seen it. It had been taken during his insubordinate career as a sailor, and I gazed up at it again with a pang. How attractive he had been with his short, strong, lightly balanced figure and springing gait. The whole shaft of his beautiful neck, his wide shoulders and deep chest, his narrow hips, everything that he had had been almost effeminately displayed by that extraordinary close-fitting costume of ribbons, bows, and silks. And what fun he had been, so lively and so gay. . . . Much water, alas, had flowed under the bridge since then. A momentary weak feeling of anger and self-pity took me at the thought of what he had been and what marriage had done to him. Boy though he still was to my older mind, the straight back was now a trifle bowed, but the face was the same and from behind the glass of the picture the limpid eyes looked down at me steadfastly, as reassuringly as they had looked from behind the glass of the visitor's booth. He had promised a happier future; they seemed to confirm the promise. It was with a feeling of refreshment that I returned to the kitchen.

I noticed at once that, in my short absence, the window had been closed. The working classes, I reflected with a shrug, have an ineradicable belief that the colds from which they constantly suffer are due to fresh air rather than to the lack of it. With such superficial mental comment did I dismiss an incident to which, I realized when I recalled it some months later, I would have been wiser to pay more serious attention, for it set in a way, the psychological pattern of much that followed. Soon afterwards I took my departure, leaving Dickie's keep behind and carrying with me a seed cake which Millie had made specially for me.

"It's Megan, Frank."

Why did she always have to begin like that, I wondered irritably; as though anyone could possibly mistake that sickening Welsh voice.

"Yes?"

"I've had a visit to Johnny."

"How is he?"

"Oh, he's well. He's counting the days, he says. It's the

evenings pass slow, that's the worst part, he says. He says could you send him some books to read?"

"Isn't there a prison library?" I asked shortly. Johnny was in Wormwood Scrubs.

"I don't know," said the voice, retreating.

"What sort of books anyway?"

"I don't know. He didn't say. He said you'd know the kind he likes."

"Oh, all right." I was slightly mollified by this admission that he and I had some private understanding from which she was excluded. "Anything else?"

"He said to give you his best." The remark jarred on me. "I'll be writing to him tomorrow; shall I give him any message?"

"Yes, give him my *love*," I said. And put that in your pipe and smoke it, I thought as I set the receiver down.

It was two months before I returned to Stratford. When my second visit fell due I had a week-end engagement elsewhere, and the suggestion that Millie might meet me at Aldgate one evening instead was declined; she couldn't leave Dickie, she said. So I sent the money by post. But a number of letters from her kept me *au fait* with his progress, the colds they all constantly exchanged, and the state of the weather. These letters, and the telephone calls from Megan, chiefly served to remind me, however, of the communication I did *not* get, wanted, increasingly missed, and regarded myself, indeed, at the very least, as having earned: a letter from Johnny. From him direct I had not heard at all.

At the end of February I took the long bus ride again. It was a fine, sharp, sunny afternoon.

"And how are all the colds?" I asked as I followed Millie down the narrow passage.

"Tom's not too well. He's been having trouble with his back."

This meant his piles, I knew. The kitchen was like an oven.

"Sorry to hear that," I said, extending my hand to him. "My nephew seems in good form anyway," I added, looking warily at the child's backview.

"He's lovely!" said Millie proudly. "What do you think of him, Frank? He looks better, don't he? See how fat and rosy his cheeks are! Look who's come to see you, Dickie-bird!"

Dickie, who had been happily engaged in beating the arm of his chair with a spoon, turned round. His wretched little face at once began to pucker.

"Now, now!" I said, putting up my arm in mock self-defense, "What's wrong with me, anyway?"

Tom chuckled from the fireplace.

"He don't mean nothing," said Millie hastily. "P'raps it's your specs," she added. "He's not used to them things."

"That's an idea!" I took them off. Dickie dissolved into tears. "Yes, it's the specs," I concluded clownishly, restoring them to my nose. But Millie seemed a bit put out, so I changed the conversation to the subject which was, in any case, uppermost in my mind, by asking: "Have you heard from Johnny."

"No, I'm expecting a letter any day," said she, coaxing the child back to good humor. "Have you?"

"No, I haven't. I've had the promise of a letter, but no letter. The only news I get of him is second-hand from Megan. She scoops the pool, it seems."

"They don't allow him much in the way of letters, poor boy," said Millie abstractedly. "That's where it is."

Her loyalty to Johnny was constant and sometimes exasperating. She too had suffered many a disappointment over him in the past, and the lovingly prepared supper, put back into the oven to keep hot for him when he was late, had often stayed there all night; yet she never could bear to hear him criticized and instantly sought round for excuses. But I was not to be balked of my prey.

"Yes, I know that; but it comes to about a letter and a visit a month, and since he's been there three months now, that's three visits and three letters at least, and she's had the lot."

"He ought to write to you after all you've done for him," said Millie, spooning bread-and-milk into Dickie's face.

"And to you for that matter. Why the devil should she get everything?"

"I suppose she thinks she come first, being his wife," said Millie placidly. "There's her condition, too."

"I'm sure she's making the most of it," I replied peevishly.

"She tells me she's going to apply for special visits on passionate grounds, and she reckons she'll get them, so we may all see and hear more of him then. She was over here last Sunday, her and little Rita, and they'd just been up to see him. What do you think of Rita, Frank?"

This was Millie's little game again; she knew perfectly well what I thought of Rita and thought the same, but did not like to be the first to begin upon her destruction. I was feeling too hot and limp to play.

"I try *not* to think of her."

"She don't have much to say for herself, do she?" said Millie with a laugh. "They're a pair! but Megan mostly lets me know before she goes to see Johnny, I will say that, and now that she's started to get open visits, as she calls them, instead of seeing him behind them windows, which I wouldn't care to do, I like to give her a packet of cigarettes to take him, which isn't allowed I know, but she manages to pass them somehow, and poor old Johnny do miss his smoke. Then she comes up afterwards and brings us the news. Give her her due she takes trouble over that. But she don't say much when she do come, and what she do say seems a bit 'eartless to my way of thinking, if you know what I mean. He looked fatter and better than when he went in, that's what she told us; but I'd have to see him for meself before I'd believe that, for it can't be 'ealthy in them 'orrid places. And he had a job washing up in the kitchen what earned him a few pennies, she said that and that she was pleased they was teaching him something useful for when he come home. But she never offered to help *me* with the washing-up, I noticed that, not that I'd have let her if she had. She's not what you'd call company, and it stands out more now that she don't have Johnny to take things off of her. I don't know if she's shy."

"What '*er*!" put in Tom from the fireplace. Millie cackled.

"A fat lot you know about it," she remarked. Then to me: "He don't take a blind bit of notice of her while she's here. He just sit and read his paper and leave it all to me."

"Is it possible you don't like her, Tom?" I asked, mopping my forehead. Millie's balanced judgments were far from suiting me and, rash though it was to draw him out, his ejaculation seemed to open up more profitable fields.

He munched on his pipe before delivering himself.

"She's sly. I sized 'er up first time I set eyes on 'er, didn't I, mate?" This was to Millie. "I always said she'd do Johnny no good."

"Hear, hear!" I applauded. "You never spoke a truer word, Tom. But what I *can't* understand is Johnny's own behavior. He was fed to the teeth not long ago with her infernal jealousy, and from the names he called her you'd have thought he positively hated her. In fact he told me once he was sick to death of her and meant to leave her. Yet as soon as this business happens he's all over her again. It's maddening!"

"Yes, you was saying she was jealous of you," said Millie encouragingly.

"Well, she's 'is wife for better nor worse," observed Tom, suddenly moody, "and you can't come between man and wife."

"*I* can!" I said pertly, for the remark seemed uncalled for.

"Ah—" began Tom; but Millie at once chipped in with: "That's enough from you!"

I was momentarily taken aback by this brief interchange, but I ignored it and put an end to the silence that followed by saying mildly: "Well anyway, I think it's time someone else got a look in; besides, I was his friend long before she was his wife."

The perspiration was now trickling down my back,

and Millie's face too, I noticed, was shiny and red. Signs of discomfort in Tom one did not expect; he did not appear to have a bead of moisture in his whole body. Dare I ask for the window to be opened? Better not, perhaps. They preferred their frowst. . . .

"Millie dear, it's awfully hot in here. Would you mind if I opened the window for a moment?"

"Yes do. I was just thinking it was getting rather warm meself, and I know you like a bit of fresh air."

"A bit of fresh air!" I thought. If I was condemned to spend the rest of a fine afternoon in this cauldron of a kitchen, I would fill it as full of fresh air as it would hold; and leaning over the huge table, which occupied about a third of the floor space, I grasped the lower sash and flung it up. The result was startling, to say the least. A sort of wolf, which must have been sunning itself in the yard outside, rose up on its hind legs and, planting its forepaws on the sill, gazed inquiringly in at us.

"Heavens!" I cried, falling back. "Don't tell me that's Johnny's dog!"

The creature was immense—or at any rate looked so in its present attitude. It was also strikingly handsome. Its light gray vulpine head was long and sharp, and surmounted by extraordinarily tall ears. The winter sun sinking behind shone through the delicate tissue of these remarkable erections, turning them shell-pink.

"She has growed, hasn't she?" said Millie.

But she had scarcely spoken when, with a single bound, Evie vaulted lightly over the sill into our midst, capsizing some tea-cups with her long bushy tail. There was an immediate outcry.

"Now look what you've done!" exclaimed Millie. "She's broke the 'andle off of one of me cups!"

" 'Ere, Evie, out you go!" said Tom, shutting the window.

"No, let her stay," I said in a smothered voice, for the animal's sociability had forced me down into a chair, where I was trying both to return her greeting and to prevent her waving tail from doing further damage.

"Let her be, Tom, if Frank don't mind," said Millie. "We'd not long put her out before you come. She's a proper turk. Now get down do!" for the dog had transferred attention to her.

"But however do you manage?" I asked. "She's so large!"

"To tell you the truth, Frank, I don't know how I do manage. And if it'd been anyone but Johnny I wouldn't have took her. Which isn't to say she's not a nice dog, for she is, and her and baby get on together a treat, don't they, Tom? You ought to see them laying on the rug of an evening, it's a picture. But oh she do make a lot of work!"

"You don't 'ave the worst of it, mate!" remarked Tom dryly.

Millie went off into one of her squalls of laughter.

"He has to line up for her meat! But I can't do everything. Evie's his job and Dickie's mine, aren't you, love? Nor he don't have to clear up after her neither! And she's a bastard! You can't leave nothing laying about, for she's sure to have it. Oh, Frank, I *was* sorry, I didn't know whether to tell you, she had that doll you brought Dickie for Christmas. I couldn't find it nowhere, and then I come across it in the yard with all its insides pulled out. Oh, she had fretted it! I was disgusted with her."

"Ah well," I said laughing. "I'm glad it amused someone, for Dickie didn't think much of it."

"He did," said Millie, without conviction. "He played with it after you'd gone."

Evie was now sitting bolt upright on one of the chairs, surveying us with the liveliest expression. She was certainly an extremely pretty dog, I had never seen a prettier, stone gray with a black tunic and her face most elegantly marked. Her nose and lips were sooty, as also were the rims of her bright brown eyes, above which tiny black eyebrow tufts were set like accents, and in the middle of her forehead was a dark vertical streak like a Hindu caste mark.

"She must be quite valuable," I said.

A crafty look came over Tom's lean face.

"Ah, she's good, she is! Johnny didn't make no mistake in '*er* case! 'E 'ad 'is wits about 'im then. 'Er puppies'll fetch ten to fifteen quid apiece, and she can 'ave a dozen and more at a time. I knows about them dogs. I 'ad to do with them in the Army. I——"

"Where on earth did he get her?"

" 'E said she was give 'im!" said Tom with a chuckle.

"And if he said so she was!" flashed Millie. "I won't have you call the boy a liar behind his back!"

Evie was now standing up on her hind legs on the other side of the room, pushing with her nose into some miscellaneous garments that were hanging on the wall.

"What is she doing?" I asked.

"Her lead's up there," said Millie. "I expect she wants to go out. She hasn't been out for a coupler days. Tom hasn't felt up to it. Why don't you take her now, Tom? Your back's better, and it's time she had a bit of a run."

"She's all right," Tom grunted. "She 'as the yard."

In the course of life, I have noticed, a number of critical turning points are reached which are only recognizable as such retrospectively, long after they are passed. This moment, I was to perceive later, was a turning point in mine.

"I'll take her," I said.

"Do you want to?" said Millie. "Johnny'd be pleased, I know. But she'll pull you over! Oh, she do pull! I used to take her meself, but I can't hold her no more. She's a demon!"

"I expect I can manage."

"Would you mind?"

"I'd like to," I replied, and truthfully; any chance to escape from this suffocating kitchen was more than welcome.

"Will she go with you?" put in Tom, with his dry laugh. "They're one-man dogs, they are."

Spiky fellow! Why was he always picking at me? Perhaps she *wouldn't* go with me, but why the jeer in his voice? It was the same tone he adopted to point his advantage over me with Dickie, and implied that if the dog too made me look an outsider and a fool nothing would give him greater satisfaction. It put my back up.

"One can but try," I said coldly, getting up.

"Have a cupper tea before you go?" said Millie. "The kettle's on the boil."

"Could I have it when I come back, dear? That is, *if* we go."

"Just as you like. I'll get the lead."

Whatever Evie's ultimate decision about going out with me might be, she was manifestly delighted to see her lead unhooked from the wall.

"Where can one take her round here?" I asked, addressing myself exclusively to Millie.

"Tom takes her down the alley into Condy Road. It's quiet there. If you turn right when you go out it's a short way on."

"Aren't there any parks or greens?"

"There's the Rec."

I knew the Rec. It was a small gritty playground with some seesaws and swings in it. Evie was now hauling me to the door.

"Give 'im my stick," Tom suddenly put in. "You'll need it to clip 'er with when she pulls."

"No!" I said. I had meant to be abrupt, but it sounded rather ruder than I intended, so I added: "I shall have my hands full without."

"You'll want to keep a tight 'old on 'er," said he. "She'll get away if she can."

This seemed hardly to accord with his other forecasts, but I could not have replied to it if I would, for I was being torn down the passage by the excited animal. I heard Millie's cackle of laughter follow me; I heard Tom's shout: "Shorten the lead! You wanter shorten the lead!"; somehow or other I managed to fumble open the front door and bang it behind me: then we were flying down the street. "Will she go with you?" I thought sardonically. Two other things were also evident: Millie had not exaggerated when she said the dog pulled, and I should not have to inquire further for the whereabouts of the alley, for Evie led me at once to the mouth of it. It was clearly her customary walk. "Led", however, is a euphemism; sprawling and panting along the pavement, her legs splayed like a frog's, she dragged me there. The notion of fat Millie taking her out was ludicrous. I tried shortening the lead. I spoke to her both soothingly and reprovingly, nothing had the least effect. Throttling herself in her collar and wrenching my arm out of its socket, she lugged me after her. The alley, when we reached it, stretched far ahead, long and empty. Pulling the wild creature towards me I unclipped her lead.

It was, no doubt, I afterwards thought, the first time in her life that she had been given her freedom outside the house. And for a moment she did not know what to do with it. Standing stock still in front of me, she stared intently up into my face. Then, with a flirt of her long tail, she was off. But not far. Just as I was thinking that, after all, it would not do to lose Johnny's dog, she came bounding back and, planting her forepaws on my chest so as almost to knock me over, licked my nose. Then she was off again. Would she answer to her name? "Evie!" I called. She instantly returned and stood looking at me expectantly. "Good girl!" I said and gave her a pat. We proceeded on our way.

She was no trouble at all. Indeed, she seemed as anxious not to lose me as I was not to lose her. When the end of the alley came in view I summoned her and she submitted to the re-attachment of her lead; but no sooner was it fixed than she resumed her wild pulling and straining. That she deeply disliked it was evident; also that she was far too excitable and impetuous to be allowed in any but the safest roads without it. Condy Road looked perfectly safe; excepting for a somnolent dog sitting outside its gate it was as empty as the alley. Presumably dogs enjoyed talking to one another, so I freed her again and took her along to effect an introduction. It was a great success. He was a male dog, very playful and delighted to meet a young bitch as silly as himself; after a little preliminary polite investigation of each other's persons and some genial tail-wagging they instituted fun and games and whirled about together like dervishes.

It was a fine afternoon and I kept her out longer than I had intended, but besides the gratitude I felt to her for having enabled me to score off Tom, I was rather touched. I was touched by her beauty, the grace with which she moved and the feeling she gave of boundless energy and vitality. I was touched, too, by the attentive, almost personal, gaze she turned continually upon me. And I was touched by her own gratitude, which sent her flying back to me from time to time as though to say "Thank you." What a wretched fate, I thought, for so large and active a beast to be condemned to that poky house and this dismal district. At the end of an hour I brought her up the alley, fastened her lead when we reached the Winders" street and was lugged back to their door.

"There you are!" said Millie cheerfully, opening it. "We wondered if you was lost. You must be ready for your tea. That's enough, Evie, your dinner's ready too."

"Come along, Evie," said Tom sharply, and the dog disappeared with him into the scullery.

"Johnny'll be pleased you took her," Millie said. "I'll tell him when I see him. You don't like sugar, do you? Now sit down, you must be hungry. I'm sorry there's not more butter, but what do you think Dickie done just after you'd gone? He picked up the butter out of the dish and started to wash his face with it, like it was a cake of soap! You should have seen him, Frank! He had butter in his eyes and all up his little nose! He looked like a Chinaman!" She was convulsed. But I too had information to impart, and a determination to impart it and put Tom in his place.

"Well, she enjoyed her walk," I said when he returned. "As for her pulling——"

"She's a bugger, isn't she?" Millie said. "Did she pull you over? She's too much for me."

"I should think so! But let me tell you something: she's perfectly all right when she's off the lead. I let her go in the alley and in Condy Road. She was as good as gold."

"Well, there," said Millie vaguely. "Fill up the kettle for me, Tom, will you. The water seems to have boiled all away. I wouldn't care to change that," she continued. "She might skip off, and I don't see myself chasing after her. I'm too fat for such capers."

"No, she wouldn't. She never goes far and comes at once when she's called. But of course she has to be got to a safe road first. I'm surprised you haven't discovered it for yourself," I said smoothly to Tom, knowing how much he hated the role of the informed. "Try it next time. It's a good tip. It takes the strain off one's arm and gives her more fun."

For some moments he gave no sign of having heard me; then he observed suddenly, in his munching way: "What she oughter 'ave is one of them chain leads. I've been looking about for a second-'and one. They nips into the neck, see, when the dog starts pulling."

"That doesn't sound very nice," I said, frowning.

"They're good, they are!" said he severely. "That's what they 'as for training dogs in the Army and the Police. It teaches 'em to be'ave. The chain nips into the neck when they pulls, see, and they don't like that, so they give over pulling."

With the memory of the eager creature enjoying her liberty fresh in my mind I said sarcastically:

"Yes, I did *just* manage to grasp what you meant.

But she's young and lively. It's freedom she needs, not restraints."

Tom Winder stared into the fire. Then he said:

"You 'aven't 'ad to do with them dogs like I 'ave. I knows about them dogs. They 'as to be trained. They're tricky. 'Ighly intelligent, but tricky. You look about you in the streets. You won't see them dogs running around loose like mongrels. They're always on them chain leads what teaches 'em respect. But as soon as they've learned oo's their master, they're yours till closing time. One man dogs they are, and they foller be'ind you like a shadder. You wait till Johnny comes out and then you'll see. 'E'll soon 'ave 'er where 'e wants 'er, and that is follering be'ind 'im like a shadder. 'Ere, I'll tell you something——"

"Come along, Tom," said Millie. "Your tea's getting cold."

"It's Megan, Frank."

"Yes."

"I saw Johnny yesterday."

"Again! You'd only just been."

"I applied for an extra visit on compassionate grounds."

"Is he ill?" I asked spitefully.

"No, it's my condition," said the voice faintly.

42

"Ah yes, of course. I forgot."

"He says to give you his best and could you send him some more books like the last lot? They were smashing, he says."

"Why doesn't he write to me when he wants something?" I asked curtly. "I might add why doesn't he write to me in any case."

"He says he'll be writing you soon," said Megan.

"I seem to have heard that one before." She did not speak. "There must be a prison library, anyway. Did you ask him?"

"I asked him. He says you're only allowed one book a week and he gets through it in a day."

"Well, if he wants anything more from me he'll have to ask me personally for it. I'm fed up with these indirect appeals. Tell him that."

"Yes, Frank. But he said he'd be writing, and he said to tell you to write to him."

"Write to him? How can I write to him when I never hear?"

"He says it doesn't matter."

"But I thought he was only allowed one letter a month and that it had to be a reply to a letter he sent?"

"Yes, but he says other letters often get through without the screws rumbling."

"Without what?"

"Without the warders noticing," said Megan with a titter.

"I see. You mean it's not certain he'll get the letters?"

"He thinks he stands a good chance."

"But it's not certain?"

"I don't know," said Megan dimly. "It's what he said to say."

"Thanks!" Writing letters that might or might not reach their destination was not my favorite way of passing the time. "Anything else?"

The voice hesitated. "He misses his smokes," it then said.

"I expect he does."

"It's the worst part, he says. I always take him a packet when I go. I can't afford to buy them myself, but his mother helps me out. I get open visits now, so I can slip them to him. But of course I can't pass many and they don't last long."

"It sounds very dangerous."

"Some of the screws—warders—are easy, but you have to be quick."

"I should have thought it a stupid risk. He'll get caught and lose his remission."

"Oh, he does his nut for a smoke. He goes mad, he says."

"Well, I don't see what all this has to do with me," I said impatiently. "Anything else?"

The voice faltered again. "He says he'll be writing," it concluded feebly.

"I'm sorry I couldn't come last weekend," I said to Millie.

"It was a good thing you didn't, Frank. Oh, I *was* queer. I couldn't have spoke to you. I lost me voice. It wouldn't come out of me, it wouldn't, not for love nor money." She began to laugh. "'Speak up, mate!' Tom kept saying. 'What are you whispering for?' 'I'm not whispering,' I says, 'don't be so daft!' 'What's that?' he says, 'I can't hear a word you say.' But I couldn't make him understand, I couldn't, no matter how I forced meself. It was like a mouse talking in me. Oh, it was a proper caper! It's the damp does it."

She was engaged in pinning a clean nappie on to Dickie. It was a Wednesday, her half-day off, and although I had not specified the actual day of my appearance when I found that the weekend did not suit me, I remembered her Wednesdays and thought it would be nice to see her by herself. So I had dashed up. She was alone in her kitchen except for the child who, possibly because he was upside down, had not accorded me his customary welcome.

"Have you heard from Johnny?" she asked.

45

"No, I haven't," I said shortly.

"I'm sorry about that. Megan told us he was going to write you. I'm surprised he hasn't wrote."

"*I'm* not. I'm quite used to his empty promises." She didn't say anything. "Have *you* heard?"

"No, he hasn't wrote me yet. I don't mind for meself, so long as I know he's keeping well, but I'm sorry he hasn't wrote to you."

"I'm more than sorry, I'm very annoyed. The best he seems able to do for me is to cadge things from me indirectly and try to set me writing letters to him which he'll probably never get."

"Yes, she told us that too," said Millie calmly. "I've just wrote him one so as not to disappoint him."

"But, Millie, it's not *fair*! Why *should* she get everything? She's not the only one who's fond of him and does things for him."

"That she's not!" said Millie. "I expect——"

"——it's her condition!" I said viciously. "To hell with her bloody condition!"

"You're a bit put out, Frank, aren't you?" said she gently, looking at me over the baby's bottom.

"Yes, I am."

"I could see it when you come in."

"It's not just that I want to hear from him and see him, though of course I do. It's a matter of principle. He

46

oughtn't to be granting her all those privileges after the way she's behaved to me."

"I don't understand you when you use them long words," said Millie placidly, turning the baby over.

"What I mean is," I began, and stopped. What *did* I mean? I felt confused, lost, like someone struggling in a maze. I tried to collect my thoughts. "Well, I mean that if things are going to be happier for me in the future, if it's to be like the old times as he's promised it will be, I want proof of it *now*. Can't you understand that? She got everything her own way before, and she seems to be getting everything her own way still. Johnny's so blasted weak, Millie, that's the trouble; she does what she likes with him; and though he says she thinks the world of me now, the little rat, and won't interfere between us again, I don't believe a word of it. People's characters don't change, and she'll be just as bad when he comes out, *unless* he starts putting her in her place at once. You see that, don't you? And the way for him to do it is to give me a share of the letters and visits *at her expense*. Now do you understand what I mean?" Millie was regarding me with a detached and rather disconcerting curiosity. "It's not that I'm jealous," I added, "if that's what you're thinking. I'm not at all a jealous person. I'm perfectly ready to accept Megan so long as she accepts me. I only want——"

"Mum, mum, mum," said Dickie.

Millie beamed all over her fat red face.

"Did you hear that, Frank? He called me 'Mum'"! He thinks *I'm* his mum now!"

"Can I let Evie in?" I asked vexedly. I could hear her out in the yard scratching and whining at the door.

"I'll let her in in a minute," said Millie in breathless excitement. I must tell you, Frank! You should have been here the other day, Sunday week it was, when Megan come over! The way Dickie carried on! It was a caution! He wouldn't have nothing to do with her, he wouldn't, not even so much as look at her, and when she go to pick him up you should 'ave *eard* 'im! 'Mum, mum, mum,' he kep' crying, 'olding out 'is little 'ands to me! He thought *I* was his mum, see, and nothing would content him till I took him from her, which I had to do in the end, for it seemed he was going to have aplopsy. Oh, he did 'owl!"

I gazed at her in astonishment. Her face was flushed, her eyes sparkled, she looked like a young girl as she narrated this episode. It was quite embarrassing.

"Did she mind?" I asked.

"I couldn't say what she thought, but she passed it off quite cool, I will say. 'Why, whatever are you thinking of, Dickie?' I says. '*I'm* not your mum.' But 'Mum, mum, mum,' he kep' crying, just like he done now, but at the tops of his voice. 'Oh, so you don't want me no more?' she says, 'you've got another mum now, is that it?' But she had to give him back in the end, scarlet in the face he was. You should have *seen* him! Oh, you *was* a bad boy, Dickie-bird, wasn't you?' She hugged him and settled him in his chair. "What do you think of him, Frank? You like him, don't you?" Her large blue eyes were fixed greedily upon me.

"Oh, he's smashing!" I said pettishly, thinking what a bore she was getting.

"See, he's looking at you! And he hasn't pulled no faces today!"

I glanced at the child, He was staring at me with a heavy, dull stare. I gave a timid smile. There was no response. I winked and pulled a funny face. The small blank eyes mooned stolidly at me. Really! I thought, it was like being gaped at by the village idiot. It was positively unnerving.

"Do you see the likeness to Johnny?" asked Millie proudly.

"Johnny!" I cried aghast. Fortunately the horror in my voice passed unnoticed.

"Oh, he is! The way he look and move his little hands. He's the spit of what Johnny was as a baby."

"Is he?" A feeling of sudden exhaustion overcame me and I sank my head in my hands. Silence fell between us.

"You miss Johnny, don't you, Frank?" said Millie, in

such a kind, understanding voice that, for a moment, I could neither speak nor look at her. Then I said huskily:

"Yes, I do. I wish I could believe he missed me."

"Of course he do. I know what he thinks from the things he's said to me about you."

"What things?"

"That'd be telling!" said Millie with a laugh.

"Millie! What things?"

"Well, he said you was the grandest fellow he'd ever met. He said he'd never had nor never could have a better friend. 'There isn't nothing he wouldn't do for me, mum,' he said. Oh yes, he thinks the world of you, Frank." I stared at my shoes. "You worry too much, my dear. That's why you're so thin. I'm sorry he hasn't wrote you yet and I expect you'll be hearing from him soon, but because he don't write it don't mean he don't think. He thinks of me, I know, but he hasn't wrote me yet neither."

I said: "I know he's all right, Millie. He's a darling. I'm sure—" What was I sure of? My head was aching and I couldn't remember. "It's she who makes all the trouble."

"Well, I'll be speaking about you to him when I see him. I'll have a lot of things to tell him then. Your ears will burn that day, I bet. Did I tell you we was taking Dickie along to him next visit?"

"Oh *are* you?" I exclaimed. "I *am* glad! Is Megan standing down then?"

"Not so far as I know. I expect she'll come too."

"But, Millie, this is *wonderful* news! How did you fix it? Did you ask her to take you?"

"*Ask* her!" said Millie grandly. "I don't ask no one's permission to see me own son! I *told* her we was coming."

"That's the stuff!"

"Why don't *you* go with her one time? You could, you know. But perhaps you wouldn't like that?"

"No, I wouldn't!" How maddening it all was! She hadn't understood a single word I'd said! Not one single word! "That's the whole point! He ought to *take away* from her and *give* to me, *give* me something for myself, letter, visit, *both*, why not? Like a token, a present, just for *myself*. It's all give and no get. They ought to make a sacrifice——"

"Mum, mum, mum," said Dickie.

"There he go again!" said Millie with a cackle.

"Can Evie come in now?" I asked angrily.

"Yes, let her in. I think she knows you're here."

There was no doubt of that! Uttering ecstatic cries, the pretty creature swooped upon me with such joy that I quickly sat down in Tom's arm-chair, partly in order not to be knocked down, partly to try to confine her emotional display to the least vulnerable corner of the room. "Evie! Evie!" I said, laughing under her affectionate lickings and

pawings, "calm yourself, do!" But it was some time before she had exhausted all she had to say. Then, while I
stroked and fondled her, she lay quietly panting with the
upper part of her body on my lap, her face thrust beneath
my jacket against my ribs.

"Is she all right?" I asked. "Her nose seems rather hot
and dry."

"She's been a bit constipated, but Tom gave her some
castor oil and she's better today."

"Perhaps she doesn't get out enough," I said. Evie had
now left me and was trying to pull her lead off the wall.

"That's what it is," said Millie. "She doesn't get out
enough."

"Has she been out today?"

"No, it must be a coupler weeks since Tom took her
last."

I stared at her incredulously.

"Do you mean the dog hasn't been out of the house at
all for two weeks?"

"It must be that," said Millie. "I keep asking Tom to
take her, and he keep saying he will, then he get stuck in
his chair and he don't."

"But really, Millie, that won't do. How often has she
been out since I last took her?"

"Well, it wouldn't be more than two or three times,"
she said, after a moment's reflection.

"Millie dear! That's over a month ago! It's not right. It's dreadful."

"Of course she has the yard," said Millie a little defensively.

"My dear friend, whatever's the good of the yard to a dog like her? It's like keeping a racehorse in a stable. No wonder she's constipated!"

"It's quite right what you say, Frank. She ought to go out more. I'd take her meself, but she do pull, she pull worse than ever. I tried one day but she pulled me over like a rolling-pin."

"Of course you can't take her. But why doesn't Tom?"

"She pull him too."

"But he could let her off the lead. She's no trouble. I told him."

"He wouldn't like to chance that," said Millie; "it's dark when he takes her." Then: "Tell you the truth, Frank, I don't think he fancies it, and I don't blame him in a way. He comes in tired from work and when he's had his tea and got set by the fire he don't feel like turning out again, specially these cold nights."

"Yes, I daresay; but someone's got to take the poor brute out."

During this interchange, Evie had been moving between me and her lead as though trying to connect us. Now she was sitting on her haunches beneath it, regarding me with a fixed, unwavering stare. The dark device in the midst of her light grey forehead was more sharply defined, I noticed. It was diamond-shaped. It was a black diamond and it had the appearance of being suspended there by a fine dark thread, no more than a pencil line, which ran back from it right over the top of her pale poll midway between the tall ears. Wolf, fox, great cat, she had an extraordinary dignity, the dignity of a wild beast, the dignity of an aristocrat. Her incongruity in this tiny working-class kitchen was quite shocking.

"I must take her myself," I said crossly. "I haven't much time."

"You don't want to do that. Sit quiet and have a cupper tea. I'll get on to Tom again to take her when he comes in."

"No, I must take her. She's asking me."

"Just as you please." Millie was disappointed. "Johnny'll be grateful, I know. I had a boy come along last week wanting to take her."

"A boy?" I said sharply. "What boy?"

"Some young lad," said Millie vaguely. "He live down the road, I think, but I don't know him."

"But what did he want? Why did he come?"

"He see her out with Tom, or something, and took a fancy to her, so he ask if he could walk her out too. A bit of sauce I thought it, but I daresay he meant no harm."

"Millie!" I cried. "You don't mean you refused?"

"Well, he was only a young lad and I couldn't take the risk of something happening to her. She's Johnny's dog and he give her to me to mind, so she's my responsibility as you might say."

"But, my dear Millie," I exclaimed exasperated, "something will happen to her if she *doesn't* get out! She'll go sick or mad. Do find out about the boy and let him take her. It's the very thing."

"I couldn't do it without Johnny's permission. I'd have to ask him first."

"He's sure to say yes."

"I'd have to ask him. Tell you the truth. Frank, I sometimes wish I'd never had her, and I wouldn't be sorry to see the back of her. Of course she's a nice dog and baby likes her, but oh she's a devil! Nothing's safe from her, and now she's took to pulling me washing off of the line! All down in the dirt it was last week when I come in from shopping and I had it all to do over again. Oh she do play me up! I daresn't leave her out in the yard no more."

"Then she doesn't even get the yard!"

"Not when me washing's up. She has to go in the scullery then."

"It's all because she doesn't get out enough. You understand that, don't you? Since she has no chance to use up her energy outside, she uses it up inside."

"It's quite right what you say, Frank," said Millie. "It's what I keep telling Tom." A sudden gust of laughter shook her. "She had Tom's slippers last week! You remember, them red ones I give him for Christmas? 'Ow she got 'em I don't know, for I puts everything out of her way when I goes out. But she 'ad 'em all right! You should have seen them when I got back! There wasn't nothing left of them!" Another immense gust. "And you should have seen Tom's face when he come home and found what she done! Laugh! You couldn't 'elp but laugh! Oh, but he did pay her for that! He took off his belt to her. 'You didn't ought to 'it 'er like that, Tom,' I said, 'it's not fair. It's your own fault for not taking her out more.' But he only told me to mind me business. Oh he did give it 'er!"

For a moment I could not speak. I was trembling with rage and indignation. Then I said violently:

"How disgusting!"

Millie glanced at me in a startled way.

"Of course he was sorry afterwards," she said in her slow voice. "I could see that. He made an extra fuss of her that evening."

"Does he beat her often?" I asked, with a sick feeling looking at the brilliant and extraordinary face by the door.

"I wouldn't say often," replied Millie mildly. "He gets a bit ratty with her at times when he's in a bad mood or

his back's been playing him up. But you mustn't go thinking Tom's a cruel man, for he's not. He's a kind man at
heart, and he's fond of her. Oh yes, he thinks the world of
her, he do."

"Just like your Johnny does of me!" I said, getting up.

It's the ears of course, I thought. They compelled, those
tall shafts constantly turned upon me, an attention they
seemed unremittingly to give. Yet was it due only to that,
this feeling I had with her again of being not merely
watched but communicated with?

Our walk had been much the same as the last, excepting that, since she was larger and, as Millie had implied,
more frantic in her excitement, the strain upon my arm
had been greater. In the alley-way, as soon as I had freed
her, she had relieved herself of an evil-looking grey por-
ridge of excrement. Then we had happened in our ram-
blings upon an extensive bomb-site; half of what had
once been a great block of council-flats had been demol-
ished, providing what seemed to be the only open space,
besides the Rec., in the neighborhood. There, amidst the
rubble and the rubbish, some stunted grass had managed
to sprout, and picking my way through the debris to the
center, where the ground was clearer, I had seated myself
upon a piece of fallen masonry and lighted a cigarette to

calm my agitation. My hands, I noticed as I cupped them round the match, were quite black from stroking the dog.

She stood before me now in the failing light of this early March evening, gazing at me intently. How pretty she was! How elegantly tailored her neat sable-grey, two-piece costume! Her sharp watchful face was framed in a delicate Elizabethan ruff, which frilled out from the lobes of her ears and covered all her throat and breast with a snowy shirt-front. She stood like a statue—no, she was too lightly poised for that; more like a dancer or—what was it she recalled, confronting me there in her spruce turn-out, compelling my attention with her still, level gaze? An advertisement perhaps? And for some reason—absurd association!—I remembered the poster of that engaging young uniformed woman who, case of Sanitas in hand, begs to be allowed to come and disinfect one's telephone. I smiled at Evie. What did she want? What was she trying to say?

"What is it, my pretty?" I asked, holding out my hand. Her tall ears at once lay back, her face took on an expression of sweetness and gentleness, and she came forward a step or two to touch it with her nose; then she retreated again, her ears re-erected, her tail moving slightly from side to side as it hung, regarding me steadily. Of course, of course, she wanted to play. I found a stick and threw it; she flew after it like an arrow and brought it back. But with a charming flirtatiousness she would not let me have it; she offered it, then with a teasing merry look withdrew the offer from my grasping hand. She was asking to be chased; I chased her, secured the stick from her jaws without difficulty and threw it again. How she loved running, using her muscles, her strong young limbs! If Tom or the rebuffed boy took her out every day round these mean streets what use would that be to her? She ought to be bounding a daily ten miles over grass. She ought to be in the country.

I played with her abstractedly, thinking of her life. Millie and Tom were both at work all day; she must be left entirely alone from about eight o'clock in the morning until six in the evening, except when Millie popped home in her lunch hour, as she sometimes did, to do a little shopping. What in the world did the dog do with herself all that time? Roll on her back in the coaldust, no doubt, from the state of her fur, to kick about in the air the legs she had no other means of using. Then at last the great moment of her day would come when they both returned home, for that would be company at least; and how she would greet them, how she would thank them for that! They would admit her to the kitchen now while they had their tea, so that she could entertain them by making a pretty tableau with baby on the hearthrug—if she had been good! But my mind recoiled from the thought of that ugly runt taking off his belt to the playful affectionate creature. Then hope constantly springing, constantly dashed. . . . She would gaze longingly at her lead on the wall, go over to it to investigate it with her black nose, employ all her little arts to draw attention to her needs, and get nothing, nothing, be told to be patient, to "lay down", which was all she ever did. . . . Day after day, day after day, nothing, nothing; the giving and the never getting; the hoping and the waiting for something that never comes, loneliness and frustration. . . . I ground out the hideous words aloud as I hurled the stick for the last time.

Heavily I returned to my concrete seat, but she did not want me to sit down, and first she had my gloves out of one of my pockets, then, when I had gratified her desire that I should retrieve them, my beret out of the other. She capered off with that, keeping a sideways eye upon me in the hope that I would pursue her again, but a feeling of such melancholy, such despair, had overcome me that I could not get up. Finding me uncooperative, she dropped it and, coming upon her stick where she had left it, suddenly began to play by herself. Pouncing upon it with an access of extraordinary ferocity, she flung it up into the air and, as it fell, fled from it with her ears back and her tail between her legs, as though it had stung her. Then, at some distance from it, she whirled about and crouched, staring at it intently. The mesmeric concentration of her gaze, the tenseness of her attitude as she lay there, like some wild beast at full length, her flat lowered head just clear of the ground, were so dramatic that I too stared at the stick, expecting to see it move. Now with infinite stealth she stalked it. Still crouching she advanced upon it, slowly, inexorably, her long sharp nose pointing at her victim, until, with a sudden bound, she leapt upon it, seized, cast it into the air, and flew fearfully from its descent once more—to begin the process all over again. I watched her spellbound, this great catlike creature playing her game of make-belief in the twiight. No doubt it was a game she had devised to while away the lonely hours in the Winders' back yard.

"Millie dear, I've just had a splendid idea. I've got a cousin down in the country, and I'm going to ask her to take care of Evie until Johnny comes out. She'll get all the exercise she needs there and you and Tom won't have the bother of her any more."

"Perhaps your cousin won't want her," said Millie after a pause.

"I'm sure she will. She's got a cottage with a garden and nothing whatever to do. She'll be delighted. And Evie will be in clover."

"Of course, she's a good 'ouse dog."

Is it because the working classes fill our prisons with thieves like Johnny that they in particular seem so often to suppose that their own miserable property requires protection?

"She's *not* a house dog, Millie," I said patiently. "She's a sheep dog. She's bred for an active open-air life and she's not getting it here."

"That's quite right what you say," said Millie placidly.

"In any case I've never heard her bark," I added.

"She do bark. I expect she knows your step. Now sit down and have your tea before it gets cold. Come, Evie" (opening the scullery door), "you've had your good time, now go and lay down."

"Don't you think it's a good idea?" I persisted. "You said just now you'd like to see the back of her."

"Oh, I don't mind for meself. Dickie's all I live for. But I'd have to ask Johnny first."

"Why, on earth?" I said testily. "It only wastes time, and anyway it's not for him to decide. I mean he's left us his muddle to cope with and we must cope with it as best we can."

"I'd have to ask him first," said Millie calmly. "I couldn't do nothing like that without his permission."

"You really think it necessary?" I asked, controlling myself. "You see if I'd accepted charge of her in the beginning, as he asked me to, it's what *I* would have done, for I couldn't have given her a proper life either. I'd have decided the matter for him. And after all, he's bound to agree when he knows the kind of life she's leading here. Also it would be greatly to his advantage for her to go to my cousin; she'd get some training there, which she's badly in need of."

"It's quite right what you say, Frank, and I'll tell Johnny when I see him. He'll be pleased at all the trouble you've took. But you see he gave her to me to mind, so she's my responsibility as you might say. Now that's enough about Evie. You've not drunk your tea yet. Have a bit of this cake. I made it specially for you. And give over worrying! It killed the cat, they say."

She was bored with the subject, I could see, and wanted to talk about other things, Dickie no doubt: but the dog's plight and silent proximity behind the scullery door continued to disturb my thoughts. When I got up to go I felt I wanted to say goodbye to her, but in view of Millie's small display of impatience I saw that it might be unwise to admit this. I asked instead if I could use the lav.

"You know where it is," said she.

Except for the threads of failing daylight that outlined the ill-fitting yard door on my left, it was pitch dark in the scullery when I had closed the kitchen door behind me. Where the electric light switch was I could not remember, and I stood for a moment motionless in the gloom. There was a slight movement on my right, a soft nose—cooler I was glad to feel—touched my hand, and Evie rose silently up out of the shadows to welcome me. I fumbled the yard door open, and she led me out with something of the air of a country hostess showing one over the grounds. It was a narrow strip of yard, a dozen paces long, perhaps half as many wide, and contained a heap of dusty coal, Tom's allotment tools and the props of Millie's washing line. At the far end was a gate, never used, on to a weedy, dustbin-cluttered passageway that strung the back yards of this row of small houses together. A long black ridge across the evening sky was the embankment of the London and North Eastern Railway.

The outside sanitation was by the gate and I thought I might as well use it. Evie had left me; I could hear her rummaging near the coal-heap at the other end of the yard. When I emerged she was facing me outside the lavatory door, gazing up at me with her brilliant black-rimmed eyes. But how very odd she looked, as though she were putting out her tongue at me! Then I saw that it was not her tongue; she had something in her jaws, something red. I stretched out my hand for it and she gently yielded it up. It was a piece of Tom's Christmas slippers, warm from her breath. She had dug it up for me from some secret hiding-place. I bent down and kissed her. Sweet creature! She, at all events, had brought me a present.

Millie saw me to the door. She was a great goose, but she was also a great dear, I thought, looking at her fat pink childish face with its rather poppy eyes. Suddenly happy, I gave her, too, a good smacking kiss.

"You won't forget to tell Johnny?"

"No, I won't forget, Frank. I'll write you as soon as I've seen him. And I'll get on to Tom again to take her out."

As I went through the gate I nearly collided with that dreary fellow returning home. Disinclined though I was to speak to him I halted for a moment and said something like: "Hullo, Tom! I'm just off. Sorry to have missed you." But he brushed past me like a ghost, so that, although I'd never suspected him of drinking to excess, I thought he must have taken a little too much.

To my annoyance my cousin in Surrey refused Evie. "I expect I should get fond of her," she wrote, "and then I should be sorry to part with her when the moment came. Besides, I don't know your friends, why should I concern myself in their affairs? I have troubles enough of my own. If it had been *your* dog it would have been a different matter." Tiresome woman! Yet I might have known. It was characteristic of her that she should be willing, even eager, to do anything for me, except be made use of; and since she frequently claimed my time and attention for the disentangling of *her* complex affairs I was incensed by her reply. She did, however, make a belated attempt to be helpful by adding that a neighbor of hers, a Miss Sweeting, ran a kennel for dogs and might be useful if I cared to communicate with her. "I have just spoken to Miss Sweeting," said a postscript, "as she happened to pass. She didn't seem keen, but says you can ring her if you like. She also said you should tell your friends that it is unwise to beat dogs like Evie, it only makes them savage. Why not come down and talk to her yourself? And to me? I am wanting advice about some investments."

After this I marked time. Miss Sweeting, presumably, would be a business proposition, and although I had no doubt of Johnny's reply, it seemed better to wait until I received it. But busy though I was in the days that followed, I found myself thinking of Evie and remembering uncomfortably the intent, expectant looks she had fastened upon me.

Millie's letter came a fortnight later. "We had a nice visit," she wrote, "though it seems we was too many only two being allowed but they did not make trouble which was good of them so we all got in and baby said 'Da da' when Johnny took him up which made a lump come in my throat, it is true what Megan said about him being fatter in the face but he did not look at all well to me and I am worry about him. He said a lot of very nice things about you and that he could never repay you for all you had done for him and would be writing you soon and he don't want Evie to go to your cousin in case she won't give her up when he comes out and, he don't want no boy to take her neither, he says that if you and Tom go on taking her out she will be all right."

This letter too filled me with indignation. That there was a certain pertinence, at any rate prevalence, about Johnny's reason for resisting my plan for Evie was unfortunately undeniable, for the same sort of difficulty that he foresaw had also occurred to my cousin; but there was all the difference in the world between *her* feeling that parting with the dog would be painful, and *his* monstrous suggestion that she might actually refuse to give her up. Did he suppose, I asked myself angrily, that my friends and I were as crooked as himself? And did he also imagine that I had nothing better to do with my time than run up to Stratford to exercise his dog? And what, finally, did he mean by "you and Tom", when the whole point was that the lazy brute was no good at all? I wrote back to Millie to say that I thought it very stupid of him to reject my plan, that I felt insulted by his reason and puzzled by the rest of his reply. If I had foreseen it, I said, I would have suggested a country kennel instead, for which I was willing to pay and to which his objection could not apply since it would be a business and not a personal arrangement. I would put this to him, I concluded, when his letter came, if it ever did, and would she please do the same if she were writing.

Millie replied promptly, as was her habit, mostly about Dickie, who had been poorly since the expedition, then about Easter, which fell upon the approaching weekend. Was I thinking of coming up to see her then? (If I reverted to schedule my next visit was, in fact, then due.) If I was, would I please not come on the Bank Holiday because they had booked seats on a coach for Margate on that day. Dickie being a bit run down they thought it would do him good. But she would be glad to see me on the Saturday or Sunday, of which I might prefer the first seeing that Megan was coming on the second. At the very end she added briefly that I was not to worry about the dog who was perfectly all right. It was the only reference to Evie in the letter which, though friendly, renewed the feeling I had had from her before that she was bored with the subject and that when she said that I was not to worry about the dog she meant, not that I was not to worry myself, but that I was not to worry her. Not that I was not to worry at all, thin though it might make me, I thought with a smile at her transparency as I read the letter again, but I must learn to worry about the right things, and her letter quietly ordered them for me. However, it was not about Dickie and his ailments that I was thinking when I put it down; I was wondering what was to happen to Evie when they all went off to Margate for the day. They could not take her with them; were they going to leave her alone in the house from early morning till late at night? Poor creature, it really was disgraceful! I picked up my pen to say that if such were the case I would come and take her out in their absence. Then I put it down. It would sound like nagging. That would be a mistake. I had better go up on the Saturday and take her out then. And could I not take her for a decent walk? There must surely be commons or parks of some kind in the district. I opened a map: yes, of course, Victoria Park. I had never been into it, but it looked fairly large. It also looked rather a distance from Millie's, but why should I not try to get Evie there? What fun it would be to set her free upon grass, to see her stretching her long limbs. . . . But such an expedition would occupy an appreciable part of the visit, an apportionment of my time that was unlikely to find favor with Millie. Instead of springing it on her when I arrived, I had better prepare her mind at once; I could invoke Johnny, of course, whose word was law—and whose wishes about running up to exercise his dog I seemed after all to be gratifying! I therefore wrote a careful letter, devoting the whole of the first page to a concern for

Dickie which, I could only hope, would appear more convincing to her than it looked to me; at the end in a short sentence I said that I would come up on the Saturday, and that I would arrive specially early in the morning to take Evie for a longish walk, "since Johnny wished it", before I did anything else.

On the Friday morning, the day before I went, Johnny's long-awaited letter came. The first noticeable thing about it was that it was far from being official. The envelope was a plain one, very dirty and crumpled, with the address scrawled in pencil. The postmark was Paddington. Inside was another envelope more carefully addressed to a Mr. Smithers of that district, and Johnny's letter. The gist of this was that one of the "screws", who was "a decent chap and to be trusted", had agreed to smuggle some tobacco to Johnny. It was to be "a good amount of tobacco, about fifteen ounces" and, considering that and the big risk the screw was taking, well worth the five pounds I was requested to put into the enclosed envelope, which should be registered. Would I then send a wire to Johnny wishing him "a happy birthday"? It wasn't his birthday, of course, but no one would know that, greeting telegrams always got through and he would understand from it that the money had been sent. I could put in a letter to him, too, which the screw had also promised to deliver. "I know that you will do this for my sake, Frank, because I only earn threepence and you can imagine how long that lasts me, and also, Frank, I will be able to go on getting letters out to you and to my mother, but remember, Frank, these must never be mentioned because as you know they are not official. Well, Frank, how are you keeping? As for myself I am okay but I wish to God it was over. I shall never be able to thank . . . Megan thinks the world. . . ." There was not a word about Evie. I tore it all up and put it in the wastepaper basket. Whatever I might be thinking of Johnny at the moment, it was certainly *not* the world.

For the first time since Johnny had left home to make a life elsewhere, I set out upon the journey to Stratford with real pleasure. It was a jolly day, though windy, and Evie and I were going to have a jolly time. As I sat with my map spread out on my knees, jotting down in the margin the names of the roads that looked as though they would get us to Victoria Park as quietly as possibly, I began to whistle. Noting my own warble I cautioned myself; it would never do for Millie to suspect that the prime interest of my visit today was not to see my "nephew" but to give pleasure to Evie. It was twenty-four days since I had last seen her.

When Millie opened the door I greeted her cheerfully

and bent forward to kiss her as usual, but—it discon-
certed me for a second—she made an odd little flustered
movement away from me, saying: "I didn't know if it was
you or Ida. I'm expecting her over for the day." But I was
not really attending; I was listening instead to something
else, Evie's whimpering cries of recognition and delight
from the back of the house, which were audible all the
length of the passage. I heard them even through the far
greater din that Dickie was kicking up, squalling in his
chair. I had an impulse to rush into the kitchen, fling
wide the scullery door and let the imprisoned animal into
my arms; but I suppressed it. There were human duties to
perform first, I knew, and in not too perfunctory a manner either.

"What's up with Dickie? I hope he's not still unwell?"

"He seemed better these last few days," said Millie
anxiously, "but he's been carrying on like this all morning. I think he must have a tooth coming through, but I
can't feel nothing."

"Let's see what Uncle Frank can do," I said gaily, and
lifted the howling little oaf out of his chair. If he had
forthwith died in convulsions I should have considered
that a just and fitting end; but the effect was contrary and
astonishing. He stopped crying at once—so that Evie's
lamentations now had the stage to themselves—and
gazed into my face with his dull, wooden stare. "There!"

I exclaimed. "How about that? Doctor Frank to the rescue! He's as right as rain!" And I kissed the child's clammy forehead.

"That's it!" said Millie beaming. "It was you he wanted!"

"Da da," said Dickie, stretching out his hands to my nose.

"Oh no!" I laughed. "That's going a bit too far! If you're his mum, it would hardly do for me to be his dad!" and I handed him back to Millie. "And how's Tom?" I asked, turning to that dismal object.

Excepting for a half-hearted movement to get up when I came in he had taken no notice of me at all. Now, without raising his face from the newspaper he was reading, he mumbled something I failed to catch. Indeed, although I did not in the least mind, for the less of anything he had to say the better, his behavior was far from polite. Millie too seemed to think so.

"I thought you was going down to the allotment?" she said, rather sharply.

"All in good time," he muttered.

Dear me! I thought. Have they been having words?

"Would you like a cupper tea, Frank?" asked Millie. "It's not long made."

Yes, I must go through all the social hoops with a good grace.

"Thank you, dear, I would."

The scullery door began to rattle as Evie scratched at it.

"Has Johnny wrote you yet?" Millie inquired as she poured the tea.

"Yes, I had a letter yesterday."

"That's right. I thought you had. I could see you was feeling more yourself directly you come in. Did he tell you about our visit?"

Should I disillusion the great gaby? No, it would be unkind. A heart-rending cry from Evie pierced my ears.

"Well, no, he didn't. It wasn't the official letter I was hoping for, and he didn't say much about anything, except that some screw friend of his was willing to smuggle him in some tobacco if I made it worth his while."

"Did you ever!" laughed Millie. "What cheek!"

"He wanted me to send the screw five pounds. That's all the letter was about."

"Five pounds! You never sent it. Frank?" cried Millie aghast.

"Well, I haven't, as a matter of fact. I didn't quite know what to do," I added mendaciously. "It seemed rather a lot."

"I should 'ope not," Millie was scandalized. "Don't you send it, Frank! Johnny didn't ought to have asked you. Five pounds! For some tobacco! Whatever was he thinking of! And after all you've done for him! Did you hear that, Tom? Johnny wants Frank to send five pounds to one of them screws to fetch him in some tobacco! What do you think of that?"

It was surprising he could hear anything through the clamor of little sharp hysterical barks that Evie was now venting, and I wondered whether it was possible that they were both so inured to her demands that they no longer noticed them. Otherwise why did they not let the poor lonely creature in? But Tom did hear the question and, morose though he appeared to be, this direct and uncancelled appeal to his wisdom was irresistible.

"Johnny must be going daft! I'd never 'ave thought 'im such a mug! You might just as well pitch the money in this 'ere grate for all the good it'd do 'im! 'E wouldn't get a pinch of 'is tobaccer, not so much as a draw. And what could 'e do? 'E couldn't do nothing. 'E couldn't even say nothing. They'd tickle 'is arse for 'im whatever 'e did. Them screws! They're a crafty lot of bastards! They was just the same in the Army. I remember——"

"Johnny didn't seem exactly confident himself," I cut in. "He wanted me to send him a wire to wish him a happy birthday. That was to tip him off that I'd sent the money."

This amused Millie:

"Well, did you ever! The things he think of! Why it's

not his birthday till November! Don't you do it, Frank!
I'm sure it's right what Tom says; Johnny wouldn't
get nothing out of it and he didn't ought to have asked
you anyway. We had one of them screws alongside of
us when we was there. Oh, he was a big feller! Johnny
said he was all right, but I didn't like him standing so
close. And Megan passed Johnny a packet of cigarettes
right under his nose! Oh dear! I felt meself go 'to all over.
I did feel queer! Do you know how she done it, Frank?
She slip 'em up under baby's frock when we handed
him over to Johnny. Oh, she was quick! I was surprised.
She never seems to have no go in her when she's here.
And what do you think Johnny said?" She went off into
one of her squalls of laughter. "He said 'Don't let 'im
piddle on 'em, for Gawd's sake!' Oh, he did make us
laugh! But he do miss his smoke, poor old Johnny. It's
the worst part, he says. And of course it's what you've
never had you never miss. And he don't look at all well,
Frank. Do he, Tom? He's fat and he's thin, if you know
what I mean. You can see he grieve." (Bang went the
scullery door as Evie rose up against it.) "When baby said
'Da da' tears come into his eyes. Oh, it did upset me! Of
course he didn't say nothing, he wouldn't want to worry
us, he joke it all off, but I bet he fret and pine, especially
of an evening." (Bang went the scullery door.) "I often
think of him shut up there all alone in his room them

long hours and have a little cry all to meself. Oh, he must feel lonely!"

Crash went the scullery door.

"Lay down, can't you!" yelled Tom suddenly from the fireside, and Evie's yelps were momentarily silenced. Then her muted appeals began again. I could stand no more. I had done my duty. I had been good long enough.

"So you're off to Margate on Monday?" I said.

"Yes, we've booked our seats," said Millie. "I hope baby will be well by then."

"Are you taking Evie with you?" I made it sound like a joke.

"That'd be a how-d'you-do!" Millie cackled. "She'll guard the house for us while we're gone."

"That's 'er job!" threw in Tom, so suddenly that I jumped.

"Aren't you going down to the allotment?" said Millie shortly. The letter-box rattled. "There's Ida. Let her in will you." Tom went out. I knew I should not ask the question, but I was determined to know.

"When did he last take her out?"

Millie did not reply. She jibbed visibly and moved over to her stove. It was almost answer enough, but I was determined:

"Not at all?"

Millie was a very truthful woman. I felt sure she would

not lie to me. But still she did not speak. There were voices and steps in the passage. Then she suddenly turned round, looked me full in the face and shook her head. Tom and Ida entered the kitchen. I had met Johnny's sister before and greeted her.

"Whatever's up with Evie?" she asked. "Has she gone daft?"

"She knows Frank's here," said Millie briefly. "Let her in will you, before she breaks me door down."

As soon as Evie entered the room my fate, which, I afterwards perceived, had for some time been in process of being drafted, was finally signed and sealed. Uttering gasping cries of joy she launched herself at me—I might have been the only person present. Then she went mad. With her ears back and her tail down she began to fly round and round the small room as though it were a circus arena. Under the table, over the chairs, under the table, over the chairs, round and round she went as fast as she could race, still making her little moaning sounds of happiness. Her body and tail thumped and banged the furniture as she pursued her headlong course; it seemed miraculous she did not hurt herself, but on and on she flew. A chair capsized, the fire-irons clattered down in the grate, Millie caught up the child into her arms, nobody spoke; we all stood gaping at the animal as she performed her wild demonstration of joy. Finally she came to rest at my feet, lay there panting for a moment, then rolled over on to her back with her legs in the air.

"Well!" said Ida, breaking the silence. "I never saw her do that before!"

I did not need the remark. It was as though the creature had given herself to me.

"Come along, old girl," I said gently, and took down her lead and collar from the wall. But this action at once brought on another surge of emotion in the excited dog, and she squirmed and coquetted and rolled to such an extent that I could not fasten the collar round her neck. When I thought it was there I found she had managed to get it, like a bit, between her teeth, and I had to begin all over again. Then she knocked my spectacles off my nose. Convulsed with laughter at her absurd antics, I fumbled blindly after them on the carpet.

" 'Ere," said Tom suddenly, "give it 'ere!" and almost snatching the collar from my hand, he grabbed hold of the dog by the scruff of her neck, forced her roughly down and, when she tried to wriggle out of his harsh grasp, dealt her a grinding blow with the heel of his hand on the bridge of her nose.

"Don't!" I cried, but it was already done. She uttered a shrill cry of pain and lay there whimpering and rubbing her nose with her paws.

"You've hurt her!" I said angrily. "She was only playing!"

"You can't 'urt a dog's snout," said he coldly, fastening the collar on to the now unresisting animal. "It's the place to 'it 'em, and she 'as to learn."

I was about to retort, when I saw Millie looking at me. I held my tongue. But I had at that moment an unpleasant, a quite frightening, feeling that, for some reason, Tom Winder hated me and that the blow he had dealt the dog had really been aimed at me.

We did not take the walk that I had planned. The direction of it obliged me to lead her at the start down one or two busy streets, and it was not only evident at once that she was in a greater state of frenzy than ever, but the cause, it seemed to me, was now apparent too. It was not merely the uncontrollable excitement of a young animal thrusting eagerly forward into freedom; it was fear. As she tore along, almost on her stomach, spurning the pavement with her powerful legs, with the motion of some beast of burden hauling a heavy load up a steep slope, she hugged the walls, keeping as far as possible from the curb. She was terrified. The racket of the road drove her against the shops; people suddenly emerging from these startled her out again towards the traffic, and she kept up a constant high-pitched barking at everyone and everything, which I had never heard her do before. It was as though the whole outside world, to which she was so little used, had thrown her into a state of nervous confusion and, totally unstrung, she tore panting through it like a demented creature, dragging me after her at a jog-trot. A bird seemed to confirm this hypothesis. The Rec. lay in our path; I set her free in it for a moment; she went to pee against the trunk of a tree, and a rook, which was roosting in its branches, uttered a brief emphatic caw and flapped its inky bulk away. Evie quailed as though a bomb had exploded and rushed back to me for protection.

Then she bit someone. I had re-attached her lead and brought her to a temporary standstill by a telephone kiosk, which afforded me shelter from the wind while I lighted a cigarette. What happened then I did not see; but behind my back some small boy approached, probably to stroke her, and she snapped at him. Whether she really hurt him I do not know; I only heard her growl and felt her lunge; but the child burst into tears and ran off holding his hand. I saw him disappear into a house nearby.

Now I too panicked. Discarding all plans I hurried her round the nearest side turning and took to my heels. One object only engrossed my mind, to remove her as quickly as possible from the scene of the crime. Without heed of direction, therefore, I rushed and bobbed along in her flying wake; my map of the district dropped out of my pocket and was abandoned where it fell; blindly I plunged down one street after another. Then, as in those terrible dreams in which we perform, always in the same recognizable yet unfamiliar landscape, our clogged and frantic labors of escape amid the ambiguities of our own fears and desires, I suddenly found myself back again on the dilapidated bombsite where we had ended up before. Too weary to unclip her lead I relinquished it from my tired hand; trailing it after her she bounded away while I stumbled over to that same concrete block that had once served me for a seat. But I had scarcely sat down upon it when she was in front of me, carrying a stick in her mouth and gazing at me with her strange animal eyes. The happiest day of her life, one of the wretchedest of mine, was to be lived over again. Her face, as she stood there challenging me, was charming; intelligent, affectionate, gay, there was no hint of savagery or ill-nature in it; and a violent gust of rage against the whole Winder family shook me, the callous Tom, Johnny the selfish, false ungrateful friend, and even fat Millie with her Margate plans for that moronic child. I thought of them shutting the door in Evie's pleading face and going off, perfectly content, to enjoy their day of winkles, baby-talk and squalls of senseless laughter while she drooled out her lonely and frustrated life in captivity. Miss Sweeting's warning had come true; their combined cruelty, ignorance, and indifference had ruined the pretty creature.

I gazed despairingly into the watchful eyes. How could I help her? Perhaps I should have taken her in the beginning . . . but how could I? . . . at least I could have given her a morning and an evening walk . . . but no, I could not . . . how could I? . . . it was impossible. . . . In the distance a train clattered and puffed away over the embankment beyond the Winders' house, and went on puffing through my head for some time afterwards. . . .

"Well, you're back quick," said Millie cheerfully. "Was she too much for you?"

Tom had gone to his allotment, I was not sorry to find. Ida was still there. I had debated on my way back whether to mention the incident of the boy and decided not to. The temptation to say "I told you so" was strong; on the other hand it could do Evie no good; improvement in her situation was not possible here. Besides, give a dog a bad name . . .

"No, but I've had a better idea. A brilliant idea! I want to take her to Barnes with me for the weekend. I suddenly thought of it and can't imagine why I never thought of it before. I've nothing special to do and it would make a wonderful change for her. The walks all round me there are far better than anything here, it would take her off your hands for the holiday and save Ida the trouble of coming in. I'll bring her back Tuesday."

"How would you feed her?" asked Millie promptly.

"That's the snag. I don't think I can. But I was hoping you'd let me take some of her meat with me. I expect you've got some laid in, haven't you?" Millie hesitated, the room blurred and I put my hand on the table to steady myself. Not another consultation with Johnny, surely! "I'd better tell you she's just bitten someone. I'm awfully worried about her."

"Bit 'im!" exclaimed Millie.

"There!" said Ida simultaneously.

I described what had happened.

"I don't believe she really hurt him, but it's the kind of thing I said would happen if she didn't get out more."

"I'm sorry to hear that," said Millie. "You do as you like, Frank. Johnny would be pleased, I know."

"Thank you, Millie."

"And you'll bring her back Tuesday?"

"Yes, Tuesday morning. I couldn't keep her a day longer. I have to go to work."

"How will you get her there?" asked Ida.

"I'm going to introduce her to a train!" I said gaily.

"Tom won't like it when he finds her gone," remarked Millie, with a cackle.

Bugger Tom! I thought. I did not say it.

It was extraordinary! It had struck me with the force of a revelation, swift, compelling, appointed, plain. At one moment I had been like a drowning man without hope; at the next, there was the life-line beside me, the way of rescue, the way of escape, the way out of the trap. Yet it had been there always, ready to be seized. How indeed could I have failed to think of it before? The train! The train! Excepting for a taxi—hard to obtain anywhere in this immediate post-war period, probably out of the question in such a wilderness as Stratford, immensely costly in any case—it was the only possible means, for a bus-conductor would be as likely to accept Evie for passenger as to accept a tigress. But the train! I had used it occasionally with Johnny in the happy past and forgotten about it since, finding the buses more convenient; it was a steam train, no lifts, no escalators; with any luck we might get a compartment to ourselves. The station was no distance off, we should be at Liver-pool Street in about fifteen minutes. Beyond that I did not look. That in itself was salvation, the firm, the gleaming shore.

But as Evie hauled me to the station in her senseless

way, a doubt assailed my mind. How was her introduction to the train to be effected? Considering her reaction to the rook, it was unlikely that she would contemplate an advancing locomotive with equanimity. Perhaps I could keep her out of the way somewhere until the train came to rest and then nip into it. I bought our tickets and made inquiries. A train was due in ten minutes; but a brief glance at the interior of the station, which was in process of reconstruction, established the fact that we could not avoid the platform. Well, there was always the waiting-room; we would huddle into that. I took her along to it. It was closed for repairs. Nothing remained for us but a bench, and seating myself upon one I clasped Evie between my legs and made soothing noises into her terrible ears. But if it was fortunate that I had foreseen the emergency at all, I had not foreseen it realistically enough. As soon as the great monster entered the station and came clanking and belching down towards us like some fabulous dragon, she made a movement of escape so convulsive that had I not had a firm hold upon her she would have wrenched her head out of her collar and fled. Instead, she sank to the platform in a quaking heap and clung to it with all her claws and force of gravity. The train stopped. I tried to coax her to it. She would not move. I pulled at her. She might have been nailed to the ground. Doors opened and slammed. I stroked her, I implored her, I slapped her; getting behind her I attempted to push her. Not an inch would she budge. Despair overcame me; even if I managed to drag her to the train, how could I hope to get her into it? I had forgotten how high the carriages were; steep steps led up to them. This then was the ignominious end to our flight; I would have to take her back to prison. The guard blew his whistle. It was the end. Then, suddenly, from the compartment in front of me, a young man sprang down to my side. "Let's lift her!" said he and, suiting the action to the word, laid hold of Evie's rump. Obediently I took her head; we raised the shivering animal between us, bundled her somehow into the carriage just as the train began to move, and fell in after her. We were off!

I have often thought since of that noble young man, that veritable *deus ex machina*, who, by lending me at this critical moment of my life an assistance which, after the episode of the little boy, I could not have requested or, if it had been merely offered, allowed, planted me firmly upon that fatal road that led to my doom. His cheerful kindness persisted throughout the short journey and was still required, for Evie, who recovered her nerve as soon as she was inside the train, had now to be endured. Excited and irrepressible, she rushed from side to side of the compartment, on and off the seats, trampling upon him, his hat and his papers, rejecting all his overtures of friendship, and barking continuously at the passing scenery, which certainly had little to recommend it. I told him something of her life by way of apology for the bad manners I could not restrain; and indeed, we both agreed, what else could be expected of a creature who was experiencing for the first time in her conscious life a room which, like the magic carpet of the fairy tales, flew and fluttered along. In this one we were left to ourselves; other travelers approached it at intermediate stops, but the apparition of what must have seemed to them an angry wolf confronting them through the glass always suggested to their minds the wisdom of discretion.

At Liverpool Street I bade a preoccupied farewell to my good genie and receded rapidly from his sight through the vaporous vaults in Evie's tow. After the appalling experience she had just undergone I decided that further mechanical transport, even if available, should be spared her for a while; But when I had suffered her drag upon my arm down Bishopsgate, Cornhill, Poultry, Cheapside, Newgate, and the Viaduct, I began to regret that considerate resolve and to look about me for help. It was not until we reached Holborn Station that a cruising taxi overtook us and the driver was bribed to carry her. Marble Arch was the destination I gave, and he set us down inside the gates at the edge of the park.

Now I had the pleasure I had promised us both, the pleasure of setting her free upon grass. And her reward

was mine. Across the open spaces of the park the rough
wind blew with its full strength, and she became a part of
the dancing day, leaping and flying among the torn trees,
wild in her delight. And her gratitude was as boundless as
her happiness. The same watchfulness, the same invitation, that I had already noticed in her governed her behavior still. Gay though she was, it was a shared gaiety
always; to caper about was not enough, I must caper too;
and who could have resisted such ebullience of spirit,
which caught one up into itself and the buffeting wind?

We crossed Hyde Park and Kensington Gardens. At the
Round Pond she launched herself at the swans and received
her first scolding: swans are dangerous. From Palace Gate,
where I had to re-attach her, to Hammersmith was another painful and exhausting stretch of pavement; but
when we reached the towing-path beyond the bridge I was
able to release her again. It was a measure of her worldly
inexperience that she should have supposed the river,
which was at the flood and level with the path, to be another shallow pond, for she rushed straight into it and
sank. The expression on her face when she rose to the sur-
face was touching in its dismay. Hastening to her rescue
I grasped her collar and hauled her out. So droll she now
looked with her fur plastered to her ribs and thighs, but
half the dog she had been, that I could not help laughing;
and this she seemed to deprecate, for she became rather

rough in her play, barging me in the back and tearing a hole in my sleeve. But the mishap was useful, for it washed much of the Winders' coal dust out of her coat.

It's Megan, Frank."

I had just finished drying Evie. For once I was not displeased to hear that toneless voice.

"Ah yes. I want a word with you. When will you be writing to Johnny again?"

"I expect to see him early next week."

"You quite live there."

"I've applied for another visit on compassionate grounds."

"No visits come my way, I notice."

"I'll tell him, Frank."

"Tell him, tell him, do. But I'm glad you're seeing him. I want to get a message to him."

"Didn't he write you? He said he was going to."

"Yes, I had a letter." There was an expectant pause at the other end. "But you know all about that." Silence. Evie was watching me intently. I winked at her. "Don't you?"

"He said something about some cigarettes," said she vaguely.

"Rather expensive ones." She did not speak. "Don't you think so?"

"I don't know," said the dim voice.

Bloody little liar! He'd put her up to it and she'd lost her nerve.

"Five pounds is a lot of money."

"Five pounds!" she echoed, with a faint giggle. "He never said nothing about that."

"It wasn't even an official letter," I said, recollecting my grievance. A stupid remark. She pounced on it.

"It couldn't be, could it? I only told him what you told me. You said he was to write you direct in future if he wanted anything. That's what you told me to tell him."

True enough! She had me there!

"Well, never mind. I want you to give him a message from me. It's important. Are you listening?"

"Yes, Frank."

"Well listen. It's about Evie. I've got her here with me for the weekend, and I'm very worried about her. I want to put her in a country kennel till he comes out——"

"His mother asked him that and——"

"I know all about that. He thought my cousin would get too fond of her. But this is different. I want to put her in a *kennel*. I've heard of a good one. It's a purely business matter, nothing personal, so the objection he had to my cousin doesn't apply. Do you understand?"

"Yes, Frank."

"It's important. He doesn't realize what's happening

to Evie. She's having a rotten life up at Millie's. She never gets out. Not at all. And she's going bad. Are you listening?"

"Yes, Frank."

"Very well. Tell him that. Millie's sick of the dog. She said so. So the country kennel will suit everyone. Will you tell him all that?"

"Yes, Frank, I'll tell him."

"And ring me up directly you've seen him."

"Yes, Frank."

"And tell him I'm waiting for a visit."

"Yes, Frank. What shall I say about the cigarettes?"

"Say I'm thinking about them."

When I had rung off I thought it would be sensible, pending Johnny's permission, to investigate Miss Sweeting's opinion and charges. She might even be unable to take Evie, in which case I would have to look elsewhere. I turned up the Surrey number my cousin had given me and rang it. A male voice answered.

"Is Miss Sweeting in?" I inquired.

"Speaking," said the voice.

"*Miss* Sweeting," I said.

"*Speaking*," said the voice.

"Oh, I'm sorry," I said confusedly, coughed and then stumbled through some explanation of my identity and trouble. I gave my silent listener an account of Evie's upbringing and circumstances, her lack of training and experience, her nervous excitability. Suppressing the incident of the small boy I merely hinted that there were indications already that she was getting rather snappy, and concluded by saying what a pretty and affectionate bitch she was. Could Miss Sweeting give me any help or advice?

"Yes," said the gruff voice, "shoot her. It's the kindest thing to do. I know exactly the sort of dog she is, had dozens of 'em through my hands. She'll never be any good now, take it from me; she'll be a nuisance to you, herself, and everyone else, besides giving the breed a bad name, which it's unfortunately got already through mishandled dogs. But don't have her injected, have her shot, it's the quickest way. Borrow a gun and do it yourself if you're fond of her. And do it at once, for you'll have to do it in the end. Though of course if you want me to take her I will; but I warn you it'll be a case of stiff fees and no results. Sorry and all that. Good-bye."

"Wait!" I cried. But Miss Sweeting had rung off.

I replaced the receiver. Evie was still sitting beside me, regarding me with such gravity that, for a stricken moment, I wondered if she could possibly have overheard. Petrified I stared into her unblinking eyes. What on earth could I do? Would that infernal woman of Johnny's report my message correctly to him? She never seemed to have a grain of sense except where her own advantage was concerned. Perhaps I had better try out on him as well one of those letters that might or might not get through. I sat down to it at once.

The daylight hours we spent mostly in the open air. Evie saw to that. And it was borne in upon me that, without perceiving it, I had grown old and dull, I had forgotten that life itself was an adventure. She corrected this. She held the key to what I had lost, the secret of delight. It was a word I often used, but what did I know of the quality itself, I thought, as I watched her inextinguishable high spirits, her insatiable appetite, not for food, in which she seemed scarcely interested, but for fun, the way she welcomed life like a lover? So extreme was her excitement when outings were proposed that it looked as though she could not bear the very thing she wanted, but, as with her collar in the Winders' kitchen, must do all she could to frustrate or postpone the fulfillment of her heart's desire. This she did by removing from me my clothes as fast as I tried to put them on, my socks, my shoes, my gloves, and bounding with them all over the flat in a transport of joy. Hysterical with laughter I would pursue her from room to room, only to find myself continually deprived again of the thing-before-the-last I had managed to retrieve. Then, when I had eventually assembled everything, she would fly into the kitchen and hurl about the vegetables from the vegetable basket, strewing the passage with carrots, onions, and potatoes as though they were flowers upon a triumphal way. She was childish, she was charming, and to me it seemed both strange and touching that anyone should find the world so wonderful.

Yet at the same time, and although it would seem unfair to criticize the character of a creature the surprising thing about whom was that she had managed to preserve any good character at all, I had to admit that she showed at once certain traits which it was difficult not to regret; she had a tendency to be both a bully and a nag. These features were constantly observable in her behavior towards the human race. Either she was nervous of people, or she simply did not like them, it was hard to tell which; at any rate not merely would she not permit them to touch her, she would not permit them even to approach or address her; from which it naturally followed, since we were always together, that she would not permit them to approach or address me. She challenged, she interrupted, she threatened, and I soon gave up attempting to take her into pubs or shops, she made such deplorable scenes. Her notion of life was perfectly clear and perfectly simple; it was to be out with me all day on the towing-path or Barnes Common and to be always on the move. I gratified her wishes in everything; it was, after all, what I had brought her away to do; but it must be added that I derived from it all a sense of personal satisfaction also, for it was a long time, I thought sourly, since anyone had seemed to want my company so much.

Whatever else might happen, it was plain, Evie was not going to let me out of her sight again. I could not go from one room of my flat to another but she instantly followed, as though fearing that if I turned a corner and her eyes lost their grip on me I might vanish quite away. When dusk fell and the curtains were drawn she accepted this, without demur, as the end of the day's play, and sat peacefully with me in my study, curled up in my big arm-chair or reclined upon the divan bed, while I read or wrote. There was, however, one quiet little indoor game with which, on the second evening, she entertained me and, to speak the truth, momentarily disturbed my mind. Not that I could have retreated then, even had I wished to retreat, I say to myself looking back; I was already too deeply involved. In any case the whole thing could easily be laughed off. . . . It began simply enough. She was sitting on the divan facing me, staring at me, her long forelegs close together, the paw joints flexed over the edge of the bed. Sitting thus, she suddenly picked up her ball which, with various other objects to which she seemed to attach a value, she had collected about her, and set it on her legs. It rolled down them, as upon rails, fell to the floor and bounced across the room towards me. This was nothing. Pure accident. Merely amusing. The mechanics were easy; our relative positions directed the ball inevitably from her to me. Receiving it into my hand I returned it with a laugh. She caught it in her jaws. But then she set it on her legs again; down them it rolled, bounced across the carpet and reached my hand. Now I looked at her with more particularity and put my book away. The ball was in my hand and she was gazing at me expectantly. For a second I hesitated, as though a cautionary hand had been laid upon me. Then I cast it back into her waiting jaws. She placed it upon her legs a third time. It did not move. Peering down at it, as if in perplexity, she gave it, with her long black nose, a shove, and it began once more its slow conversational journey from her to me. But now, just as it reached the verge—was it simply because she childishly felt she could not after all bear to part with it, or because the hitch that had occurred had vexed her?—she suddenly seized it back with a swift, almost scolding, thrust of the head and replaced it on her legs. It rolled. It fell. It bounced. It crossed the room and came into my hand. Yes, yes, of course. I know;

it is absurd to read too much into animal behavior, and afterwards, as I have said, I laughed it off; but at that moment I did take the uncanny impression that, in a deliberate and purposeful way, she had gathered up all her poor resources and, in order to reach me directly and upon my own ground, had managed to cross that uncrossable barrier that separates man and beast. The expression on her face contributed to this fleeting illusion. Some animals have a furrow above their eyes very like that furrow, etched by a lifetime of meditation, that we see upon the brow of sages. In the animal's case, of course, it is merely the loose skin wrinkling upon the line of the socket bone; but it often imparts to their faces a similar look of wisdom. Evie had this "intellectual" line, and it lent to her expression now an appearance of the profoundest concentration. With her nose pointing down and her ears cocked forward she followed, with the utmost gravity, the progress of the ball as it traveled down her legs, fell over the edge, bounded across the carpet and reached my hand; then, without altering the bent position of her head, she raised her eyes beneath their furrowed brows to mine and directed at me the kind of look that two scientists might exchange after successfully bringing off some critical experiment in physics. Yet, when I returned the ball to her now, it was as though the effort she had been making—if effort it was—suddenly failed; she became a mere dog once more, kicking up her legs and rolling about with the toy in her mouth; and when I offered out of curiosity, to replay the game next evening, I could not get it going; she seemed worried and confused; the inspiration, having done its work, had apparently gone out of her for ever.

But if I could not refix her attention upon that, her eyes seldom left my face. Throughout the evenings as we sat I was conscious always of her presence; looking up I would find her gaze upon me, and each time I would be struck afresh by the astounding variety of her beauty. The device in the midst of her forehead had altered again; perhaps her ducking in the river had exposed detail which coal-dust had hitherto obscured; the black caste mark was diamond-shaped still, but deep shadows had now developed upon either side of it, stretching across her brow, so that in certain lights the diamond looked like the body of a bird with its wings spread, a bird in flight. These dark markings on her chalky face—the diamond with its winglike stains, the oblique black-rimmed eyes with the small jet eyebrow tufts set like accents above them, the long sooty lips—symmetrically divided it up into zones of delicate pastel colors, like a stained-glass window. The skull, bisected by the thread, was two oval pools of the palest honey, the center of her face was stone gray, her cheeks were silvery white and upon each a *patte de mouche* had been tastefully set. Framed in its soft white ruff, this strange face with its heavily leaded features and the occasional expression of sadness imparted to it by some slight movement of the brows, was the face of a clown, a clown by Rouault.

Then she would move and be something quite different. She might sit in the attitude of the Sphinx, with her thick fur collar flounced upon her shoulders; or she might lower her head to rest it on her outstretched paws, so that, lying there, long and flat, the ears invisibly laid back against the dark upcurving neck, it resembled the head of some legendary serpent; or she might recline on her flank with one silver arm extended, the other doubled up upon its knuckles, in the posture of those heraldic lions that have one paw resting on an orb; or she might make herself so small and compact, withdrawing all her legs beneath her and coiling her long tail close around her, that, with the shaft of her neck rising out of the pool of her body, she looked more like a doe than a dog. I would glance up and meet her gaze which I felt to be upon me, and instantly the tall ears would crumple back and an expression of such sweetness come over her face that it was impossible not to go and caress her, this charming Krishna beast with her caste mark and her long almond eyes. I would have to go to her; she would not come to me. All the fawning sentiment that had characterized her puppy days had gone. Her love was now aloof. I would call her but she would not come. Motionless as a carven image she would sit, her head drawn back, her glowing eyes fixed tenderly and steadfastly upon me, and I would put my book away and go to her, moved by her love and her beauty. Shoot her indeed!

At night she slept as she pleased, in an arm-chair in my bedroom, or on my bed. If she began on the chair she usually ended up on the bed. It was a double bed, and sometimes she would curl up at my feet, but mostly against the pillow, laying down her head beside my own. She was quite odorless; the faint sweet smell, perhaps, of fur or feather. And when the room was darkened she fell asleep at once. In the morning she would wake me by dabbing a paw on my face; sometimes I would be roused to find her lying with all her length upon me, her forearms on my shoulders, looking gaily down into my eyes. Another day had begun. . . .

Saturday, Sunday, Monday . . . the weekend slipped away. Tomorrow I would have to take her back. I could keep her no longer. "I must make a plan," I said to myself as I turned out the light on the last day. "I'll think it over before I go to sleep." But I did not think it over; my mind seemed unable to grasp the fact and I fell asleep without

considering it at all. "I must make a plan," I said to myself the following morning as I drank my tea. "I suppose
I'd better ring up Liverpool Street and find out about
trains." But I did not. The morning was bright and beautiful; I stared through the window instead at the boats
passing up and down on the river below. Separated from
me now not merely by distance but by the memory of
that nightmare journey—for that was the obstacle my
thoughts gripped on—Stratford seemed as remote as the
Hebrides, and to get Evie back to it required, in my imagination, a resolution so dauntless, an effort so stupen-
dous, that I could not even begin to think how it could be
accomplished. Conversely, now that she had entered into
my life, that other inconceivable proposition, as I had
once envisaged it, of keeping her there, appeared, although it had not yet been put to any test, less impracti-
cable. My mind, indeed, if it could be said to be busy at
all, was busy with that. To leave her behind in my flat
was out of the question. I had deserted her twice on
Saturday to do a little shopping, and the change in her expression from jubilation as she bounded with me to the
door, to the most poignant dismay and despair when I
shut it in her face, had upset me so much that, tired
though I was, I had rushed like a madman from shop to
shop, muttering audibly at the slowness of other cus-
tomers, even in one shop earning a rebuke for trying to

push in front of them. On neither errand was I gone more than fifteen minutes, yet to my fond and guilty mind they had both seemed interminable. When I returned she was still standing where I had left her, her forehead against the door. . . . But why make plans? My office, after all, was on the way to Liverpool Street. . . . I could as easily ring up from there as from here. . . . I had a room of my own . . . no harm in trying. . . . I could always take her on if it didn't work. And I could cover myself against all eventualities by phoning a wire to Millie. This, at least, so far as planning went, was no sooner thought of than done: I said we might be delayed and she was not to worry if we did not turn up today. Perhaps she should have a letter of explanation too, just in case. . . . She would get it in the afternoon if I posted it now. I sat down to it at once, and my pen positively flew along as though the letter had been written for a long time in my head and was only waiting to come out. I described everything that had happened since I left her, the frightful journey, the walk across the parks ("If you could have seen her delighting in her youth and strength you would have understood more clearly what I mean about the wretched life she's been leading and how frustrating it is"); I told her what Miss Sweeting had said and that I was now asking Johnny through Megan to let me put Evie in a kennel until he was free ("I'm sure he'll agree. Since he's a prisoner himself and knows what loss of freedom means he would not be so cruel as to condemn his dog to a similar fate"); and I ended by saying that Evie was still so intensely nervous that I doubted whether I should be able to induce her to enter another train just yet ("If I can't I must try to work her into my life for a bit longer, though I don't at the moment see how. But she's in good health, so don't worry, and I'll be writing to you again soon"). Besides being too quickly written, this letter was far too long; I realized that when I took it to the post. Millie was no great reader and used to find, I remembered, as much difficulty with my normal calligraphy as she found with my normal speech; but I had been too carried away to think of using the special childish round-hand I generally employed when writing to her.

As soon as I had done all this I felt extraordinarily light-hearted, almost light-headed. Nothing was resolved, but some tension had been released and it was in the blithest spirits that I set out with Evie, like Dick Whittington and his cat, to walk to London. In my despatch-case I carried a few biscuits to sustain her while I worked and a tin receptacle for water. But I had not gone far before I was annoyed and perturbed to find that the joints of my legs were painfully stiff. I had, after all, covered during the weekend as great a distance as I normally walked in months. When we reached Hammersmith

Bridge I looked hopefully about for a taxi to carry us at least as far as Palace Gate; but to walk I had set out and to walk I was obliged. My objective was Gladstone House, a large block of government offices in the neighborhood of Regent's Park; my own room was on the topmost floor, the sixth. Limping into the vestibule two-and-a-half hours later I gazed longingly, though doubtfully, at the lift. . . . Surely Evie, who had been using the one in my block of flats, could be said to be lift-minded by now? But, alas, as I feared, there was to her all the difference in the world between a self-operating lift that carried no one but ourselves and went non-stop to our destination, and one that not only contained a suspicious stranger in the person of the lift-man, but took on other suspicious strangers at every floor. When we reached the third, with half a dozen nervous people aboard, and I saw another half-dozen waiting to get in, I realized that it was time to get out, that no one would attempt to detain us if we did, and that the lift-man would not feel offended if Evie never used his lift again.

The working day, which had begun so fatiguingly, ended no better. I had entertained a hope that the six-mile walk which had almost worn me out would tire Evie a little too, and that she would be disposed to lie down and doze while I attended to my correspondence. This proved the fondest of illusions. She prowled restlessly about, whining and complaining, or stood staring at me as though she could scarcely believe the evidence of her senses; she uttered loud sighs or even louder cavernous yawns, subsiding from time to time into a heap on the floor, with a startling thud, as much as to say 'Oh hell!', only to get up again immediately; she tried, by all her usual tricks of stealing and pretending to destroy my gloves, to draw attention to herself and her wishes; when this did not work she instituted noisy cat-and-mouse games with her biscuits (none of which did she actually eat), hurling them all over the carpet until it was littered with their fragments; and she barked violently with her excruciating bitch's bark, not only at everyone who entered the room but at every footstep in the busy passage outside. When I cuffed her in exasperation she put her fore-paws on my desk, upsetting the ink on my papers, in order to lick my face forgivingly. She was nevertheless much admired by my colleagues and had, for a time, a novelty value even beyond the department, so that a number of curious sightseers arrived throughout the morning. But she received them all so ungraciously that they did not call again.

Although I had considered the question of *her* lunch (needlessly, as I have said) I had given no thought to my own; when the time for it arrived the prospect of obtaining any was not bright. I could not take her into the canteen, nor could I leave her shut up for half an hour while I visited it myself. Her feelings, and mine, apart, my room had no key, and anyone might look in on me in my absence.... My only chance, it seemed to me, and it involved further physical strain, was to find some small, unfrequented pub which would provide me with a sandwich and a pint of beer. Evie's intense, petrified anxiety when she saw me preparing to leave, the almost mad stare with which her starting eyes pierced and searched my own for the answer to the only question in the world: 'Me too?', unwelcome though it was, touched me as it always did. It also affected me with a sensation of hysteria similar perhaps to her own, a feeling that if I did not take care I should begin to laugh, or to cry, or possibly to bark, and never be able to stop, for I knew that as soon as I settled the matter by clipping on her lead I should be practically raped and then sucked down the spiral staircase like a leaf in the wind. These prospects afforded me so little pleasure in my present state of fatigue that I considered letting her follow me down uncontrolled, but I was afraid she might spiral impetuously out into the dangerous road and be run over. A number of staid officials plodding up from the floors below shrank against the wall as we sped past.

The expedition was more rewarding than I had dared hope. An almost deserted pub on the far side of Regent's

Park supplied me with what I most needed, a couple of pints of refreshing beer, also with a plate of meat-and-two-veg. which I shared with Evie. On our return I decided to let her mount the stairs by herself, for she could not very well spiral out of the roof; and the experiment was interesting in that the twisting staircase seemed to make her as giddy when she was off the lead as it made me when she was on it. She started off with such speed that I wondered whether she might not acquire a permanent curve in her backbone; but the curve she did acquire was in her mind, for when she reached the landings she constantly lost her sense of direction and, circling still, came flying down again without stopping, so that I was forever meeting and parting from her, gaining her, as it were, only to repel and lose her once more.

The success of the break ended there. The afternoon passed much as the morning had done, excepting that I was left more severely alone. My outgoing mail, such little as I managed to write, was not collected unless I placed it on the mat outside my door where the incoming mail was now deposited, for the post-girls were too scared to come in. Even so, Evie heard their timid steps and never failed to issue her warning. I left early and, having once more negotiated Baker Street, Hyde Park, and Kensington Gardens, had the good fortune to find a taxi at Palace Gate to convey us to Hammersmith Bridge. Evie, when we reached home, was as fresh as a daisy; I was not; but strenuous though the day had been I derived retrospective satisfaction from it nevertheless; at any rate I had brought her through it; she had been initiated into my working life, and, meeting her strange gaze as she reclined on the bed, I told her that I hoped she had learnt a rope or two and would do better on the morrow.

When she woke me I heard a pattering on the roof. The weather was another thing I had omitted from my calculations. What on earth should I do now? Perhaps the rain would stop by the time I was up and dressed. On the contrary it was coming down harder than ever. I knew from experience that one phoned for taxis in vain. I phoned, in vain. Buses were out of the question. How could I walk her to London in this downpour? I stared at her alert, expectant face in dismay. At the base of her ears, in the openings, I noticed, the system of head hair began in a kind of spray. It was as though she had a light gray flower, a puff-ball, stuck in front of each.

"You little bitch!" I said crossly.

Then I remembered the Metropolitan Railway in Hammersmith, which I seldom used, though what I regarded as its cynical humor always entertained me when I did.

Fair promise, foul reward! After luring one on with the offer of a choice of stations romantically rural in their names—Royal Oak, Goldhawk Road, Shepherd's Bush, Ladbroke Grove, Westbourne Park—it then ushered one through some of the ugliest and grimiest districts of Central London. But it presented me with a practical solution now; Hammersmith was a terminus; there were no complications of any kind; a train was always waiting, level with the platform, and it would take us direct to Baker Street. When the rain had abated a little we set out.

Evie behaved abominably. I removed her from the train at Royal Oak, I could no longer endure her piercing and violent challenge to everyone else who got in, nor the cold looks and indignant mutterings cast at me from the other end of the compartment where the rest of the passengers huddled. Why, oh why, I asked myself as I took the intolerable creature out and walked her on through the rain, did she have to go on like that? The same thought recurred to me in my office throughout the day. So obviously brimming with intelligence, so fond of me, why, why, in spite of everything I said to her, did she seem unable to understand that my director and other members of the staff, with whom she saw me constantly in conversation, were therefore friends and could be permitted, they at least, to enter my room without being repeatedly threatened? Before the day's work was half done she had reduced the whole department to a palpable state of nerves. In the afternoon, in extremity, I fell upon her with an exclamation of rage and gave her the soundest biffing with my hands that she had so far received from me. For a moment she concealed herself beneath my desk; then she emerged and stood looking at me with an expression of such sorrow and, at the same time, such dignity, that, falling forward upon my letters, I sank my head on my arms. "Evie, Evie," I said miserably as her nose pushed in against my cheek, "what are we to do?" But I knew the answer already. I could not go on. I could not bear another day. I had had enough. The strain and the worry were too great. Her meat was finished and mine too, for I had given her my week's ration; how could I shop for more? She would have to go back to the Winders in the morning.

Did she sense that decision? She seemed particularly quiet that evening, gazing at me with her longest and her fondest looks. "Forgive me, sweet creature," I said. She had, indeed, I knew, lavished upon me in these five days her love and care; according to her notions she had done her best to entertain me and guard me from harm; she had been a good companion.

The course of betrayal is often made wonderfully easy.

Everything conspired the following day to smooth my guilty path. After phoning a wire to Millie to expect us, I started off early and walked Evie all the way to my office—the last long walk she would get for some time—to glance at my letters. When I descended with her to search for a taxi, one cruised towards the entrance of the building as though it had been ordered. At Liverpool Street a train was waiting for us. It was quite empty. Evie got into it without hesitation. No one attempted to board it at any of the other stops. She herself stood silently on the seat with her back to me looking out of the window as though trying to recollect something that had happened before. We were at Stratford in a trice. On the way back to Millie's she did not pull as much as usual; when we reached the house she turned automatically in at the gate.

Millie opened the door; and it was instantly evident that something was wrong.

"Come, Evie," she said, frustrating the dog's attempt to greet her. Of me . . . she took no notice at all. Uninvited though I was, I followed them down the passage. To my surprise, for he should have been at work, Tom was in the kitchen eating some fish. He took no notice of me either. Dickie, presumably, was with his minder.

" 'Ere, Evie," said Tom, getting up with his plate in his hand, " 'ere's a bit of fish for you." Evie slunk under the table. "Come on, old lady," he coaxed her. She remained where she was. With his disengaged hand he lifted the heavy plush tablecloth. Evie's eyes shone greenly up at him out of the gloom. This was humiliating and provoking. "Go on in!" he exclaimed vexedly, moving round the table to drive her out; and with the way to the scullery now clear, she slid into it. Tom followed her and shut the door. Millie went over to her stove. I was not invited to sit down.

The silence became oppressive. I punctured it.

"The journey was easier than I expected." Millie, her back to me, made no reply. "I hope it hasn't put you out, my keeping Evie longer than I said?"

With sudden determination Millie spoke:

"You know what I think and I haven't nothing more to say. You promised faithfully you'd bring her back Tuesday and you've broke your promise and I won't never trust you again and we don't want no more help from you."

I looked at her in a consternation not unmixed with guilt. She was scarlet in the face.

"Promise? I made no faithful promise. I said I'd bring her back Tuesday; then I thought I'd keep her a bit longer and told you so. Does it matter?"

"Yes, it do matter. And it's no good you trying now to make it seem it don't. You took her under false pretenses."

"My dear Millie! What *are* you talking about?

Haven't you had my wires and my letter explaining the difficulties?"

"Yes, I got your wires and your insultin' letter. Since you think this 'ouse is 'orrid and nasty and not fit for a dog to live in, I don't know how you can set foot in it yourself, and you're not called on to do so no more."

She was clearly extremely angry and, I thought, close to tears.

"I'm sorry if I've upset you," I said mildly. "But I must say I don't see how. I've certainly never insulted you intentionally. I've only been thinking of the dog's good, I've kept you informed and, after all, I've brought her back."

"Yes, but only after I wrote you like I did."

"Wrote me? I've had no letter from you."

"Yes, you have," said Millie, on a less confident note.

"Millie dear! Don't call me a liar. I've had no letter from you at all."

"Then why have you brought her back just now?"

"Because I couldn't keep the poor creature any longer. I told you in my letter that I was afraid she'd be too much for me." Her angry gaze examined me incredulously still. "When did you write?"

"Yesterday."

"I left my flat early this morning, before the post came."

But she had gone too far to retract.

"Well, you'll find it when you go home, and I don't

114

take back nothing that I said in it. You promised you'd bring Evie back Tuesday, and you not only broke your promise but you wrote me an insultin' letter what has hurt my feelings very much. I know my Johnny's in prison without you keep throwing it in my face, but I won't have you nor no one call him cruel, for a more tender-'earted boy never lived as never 'urt a animal in his life, and Evie was quite all right here too in this 'orrid house, well fed and well looked after——"

"My dear Millie," I interposed irritably, "I know that perfectly well, and I've never said anything different. All I said was that she was never taken out, and that it wasn't right. And you yourself agreed it wasn't right. And if it wasn't right it was wrong. And since Johnny knows that his dog never goes out——"

"Well, he don't know," said Millie defiantly, "for he wasn't told. Tom told him different."

Silence fell upon this statement.

"I see," I said at last. "Tom lied to him."

Millie flushed and turned away.

"Call it what you like. There wasn't no call to worry the boy. He's got plenty enough to worry him already."

"He'll have plenty more," I remarked dryly, "when the dog bites the baby."

Tom re-entered the room and, without glancing at me, sat down in his arm-chair. His face with its leaden coloring and hollow cheeks looked even uglier than usual. That they were both waiting for me to go could not have been more obvious. Reluctant as I was to leave matters like this, what could I do? It was, after all—their silence conveyed it as eloquently as speech—none of my business. What held me a little longer was simply the closed scullery door. I looked at it and a feeling of physical sickness seized me. She loved me and I had given her up. Could I ask to say good-bye to her? But I was frightened. The anger in the room frightened me. There was nothing left but to say good-bye to them.

"Then I will go," I said. "Good-bye."

Millie had the grace to say good-bye too, though without turning around. Tom said nothing. Neither of them saw me to the door.

Millie's letter was waiting for me. I picked it up and went into the kitchen. On the floor was Evie's water-bowl and the vegetable remains of her dinner of yesterday. I emptied and washed both the dishes and put them away. The place was as silent as the grave. On the way to my sitting-room I trod on something in the passage. It was a carrot. A feeling of the deepest dejection overcame me, and I sat for some time motionless in my chair, Millie's letter unopened in my hand. Then I read it.

Frank,

I received your letter, part of which was insult-
ing, you came here on Saturday and said that as you
had some free time, you thought it would be a good
idea to take Evie for a weekend with a promise that
you would bring her back on Tuesday, *you have not*
only broken your promise to me, but betrayed my
trust in you, Evie was quite happy here too, and for
6 months I have fed and looked after her and all
through the cold winter weather Tom has not only
lost time from work but has gone and lined up in
the cold for her meat and now that she has grown
into a fine bitch and we have got her free from
worms, you come along and take her from us, *but
she has got* to come back. My son who is the owner
of the dog, gave her to me to look after, until he
could look after her himself and said that no one
was to have her, also you got Evie up there and you
can bring her back to Stratford and to the life in my
house that is so dreadful. And lastly I know only too
well that my son is in prison without you throwing
it in my face and you are wrong, he loves animal as
much as his children and would not dream of having it shut up, like he is himself. I am very annoyed
over this affair, but it is not the first time your hor-
rid words has made a lump come in my throat, I

shall be home at 12 o'clock Thursday when I shall expect Evie.

Millie.

And 12 o'clock Thursday was the very time I had taken her back. No wonder Millie had thought it cause and effect! What a good thing I had not received the letter first—if she believed I had not. But the genuineness of my denial had impressed her I felt sure. A barge passed silently down the river across my window, as though drawn by an invisible thread. . . . How quiet the flat was, unbearable. . . . I trailed aimlessly back to the kitchen and trod on the carrot again. With a sudden howl of rage and pain I picked it up and hurled it into the dustbin. Bloody cheek, treating me like that! And after all I'd done for them! Stupid people, ignorant and obstinate, daring to assert themselves against me! Anyone would think I'd been trying to steal the blessed dog. Tom was at the bottom of it, of course. "Tom won't like it when he finds her gone." What a pity I hadn't taken her back Tuesday. Millie had been on my side then. Now she wasn't. Tom had fussed her up. "False pretenses"—he'd put the phrase into her head I was sure. "What did I tell yer? 'E don't mean to bring 'er back. 'E took 'er under false pretenses. You didn't ought to 'ave let 'er go, mate. You won't never see a 'air of 'er no more. 'E 'ad 'is eye on 'er from the start."

I could hear him saying it. "Val'able bitch"—but no, they couldn't have thought! It was too monstrous! Johnny had offered me the dog in the first place, and had sanctioned my taking her out since. What did it matter to them if I took her for a walk or a week? She wasn't *their* dog anyway, and—Millie must know it—Johnny would be delighted for me to have her for as long as I wished, especially considering. . . . But of course he didn't know! They'd lied to him, or Tom had! And Millie had let the lie pass! "There wasn't no call to worry the boy." But that wasn't the reason at all; it was to save Tom's ugly mug. "If you and Tom goes on taking her out," Millie had quoted in that earlier letter. Yes, that was it! He'd promised to take her out and then been too idle to do so, but he'd pretended he was doing so all the same! How disgraceful! How wicked! And he'd had the impertinence to call Megan "sly". And honest Millie had connived at the lie! But she'd been ashamed! She'd gone as red as a turkey cock! What a crew! So Johnny had no notion what was happening to his wretched dog! But he'd know when Megan saw him and gave him my message. Today was Thursday; she'd probably been already. Well, we would see. . . . Meanwhile what was I to say to Millie? For Evie's sake I had better be careful. Indeed yes, what a pity I hadn't taken her back on Tuesday. Yet I would have kept her even longer if I could! The letter misted over as I gazed at

119

it. I would have kept her for ever, for ever and ever. . . .
But they were not to know that. . . .

Dear Millie,

I found your letter waiting for me when I returned. I'm so sorry to have upset you by keeping
Evie a little longer than I said, but I did not think
it would matter. I knew that Johnny would be grateful to me for giving her the exercise she needs
and which you can't give her and Tom won't, so
I thought you would be pleased too, the more so
since you often say she is such a nuisance. I never
intended to insult your house. I only said it was bad
for her to be shut up in it, just as it would be bad for
her to be shut up in mine. And I see now that I was
wrong to find fault with Johnny, since it seems that
he was not told the truth. I can say no more than
this, and I shall, of course, respect your wish about
sending no further help.

yours sincerely.

Dear Frank,

thank you for your welcome letter which I received safe this morning, I am entirely to blame for
going off at you like I did and I am very sorry indeed
and hope you will except my apology, Dickie is not

at all well, I should have taken him to the doctor to-day but he seemed so queer as he has a cold and also two more teeth nearly through the poor kid is having a tough time, one side he has like a large egg the side of his face, I have got flannel with camforated oil on it around his throat also enough medicine until Monday. I hope you are keeping well this changeable weather.

all the best and love.

Not a word about Evie! I noticed that at once. Well really! The easy retraction took me aback almost as much as the angry accusation had done. A few days ago I had been practically turned out of their house for a thief and a liar; now, as though nothing of any consequence had occurred, peace was blandly restored, and presumably cash too! I read the brief note again. Dickie and his revolting lump! And not a word about Evie! This lack of reference to the subject of the dispute troubled my already sore mind like an irritation. Not that any news of her that might have been vouchsafed could have afforded me the smallest satisfaction; I could guess about her, alas, all that could be told; but the fact that she was not mentioned affronted me. Was the controversial subject now closed? Was I being tactfully warned off? The equation was wonderfully simple, I thought, glancing over the letter for the third time: now that we've got the dog safely back under lock and key, we—and you—will say no more about her! Was that the medicine I was expected to swallow? If so, they would soon find out their mistake! But why hadn't Megan phoned? This was Saturday; she must have seen Johnny by now. Had she given him my message? Or—what did she know about all this? She was there, of course, when the lie passed. Perhaps she had not liked to give my message after all; it would automatically expose Tom. Was it not possible—the suspicion flashed upon me—that they'd got at her? Now that I came to think of it she'd visited them on the Easter Sunday after she'd phoned me; it would be natural for her to mention my new plan for the dog. Could they have meddled, to save their faces? "There's no call to worry the boy. The dog's perfectly all right." Had they said something like that to her? No doubt there was a conspiracy and Megan hadn't given Johnny my message at all! Repugnant though the prospect was, I had better go and see her.

The inadequate, stained rep curtains were pinned across the front window as usual, to prevent the nosey from looking in—and Johnny perhaps from looking out, for he once told me that if ever he stood, even for a moment, gazing into the street, Megan would be sure to say "What are you sticking out your eyes at? A skirt, I suppose." If he ignored her she would come to inspect, and woe betide him if some girl did happen to pass just then, for, protest as he might, he would not hear the last of it for the rest of the day. Outside the house little Rita, aged five, was mincing and posturing up and down the pavement with a doll in her arms, engaged in some private game of make-belief. Whose daughter she was was plain enough; both she and her twin sister Gwen, now fortunately removed to their grandmother in Cardiff, had inherited not only Megan's features and coloring, but also, it seemed to me, the low cunning which, when they were all together, appeared to unite them in a silent conspiracy.

"Is your mother home from work?" I asked as I passed. Megan, I had gathered from Millie, was helping some crony to run a café somewhere in the Fulham Palace Road. Little Rita studied me for a moment with a dirty finger in her mouth (the wide-eyed stares she bestowed had nothing of the village idiot look of her brother's), then shook her head. Blast! I thought; should I go home and return later or hang about? Perhaps one of the other tenants would know when she might be expected back. I mounted the steps and rattled the letter-box. Megan opened the door.

"Oh, it's you," she said, with a faint smile, standing aside to admit me. "I was just thinking of phoning you."

"Your daughter said you were out," I observed sourly as I passed in.

"I can't do nothing with her," said Megan complacently. *I* could do something with her, but I did not say so.

Whatever else might be dubious about Johnny's wife, there was no question of her condition, I thought with a shudder as I followed her into the front room. It stuck out, as the saying is, a mile. Doubtless the business of creation was a solemn, a sacred, affair; but if I could think of it at all in such terms, I could only think of her as full of another little Gwen-Rita or another Dickie.

"I was just having a cup of tea," said she. "Would you like some?"

I declined stiffly. It was one thing to call, another to accept hospitality. The room, always scantily furnished with such odds and ends as Johnny had managed to add to the marriage suite that Millie had given him and the few objects that had come from me, was even barer than usual. The large clock with which I had presented him soon after he set up house, in the vain hope that he would sometimes glance at its face when he had an appointment with me, the wireless set, the Crusader who turned out to be a cigarette lighter and the metal goose that turned out to be a clothes brush, the gilt mirror and two hideous ornament vases, had disappeared from the mantelpiece and were no doubt back together where they frequently resided severally, in the pawn shop. On the other hand, a photograph of myself that had once held a prominent place until Megan contrived to mislay it was again on exhibition. It was, or had been, a jolly snapshot of myself and Johnny in his naval dress, which I had had enlarged and framed for him. The frame was now occupied by a repulsive colored photograph of Dickie, and I, Johnny cut away, was stuck into a corner beside him. Restoration could hardly go further; clearly Megan thought the world of me now.

"Sit down," said she in her toneless way, indicating Johnny's easy chair. I chose an upright one by the table, as signifying a more formal visit and, removing with my finger-nail some congealed baked beans from its seat, placed myself on that. Megan resumed her chair and teacup by a small flickering fire.

"How are you?" I asked frigidly.

She shrugged:

"Not too bad. It's dull on your own, you know." What did she mean by "you know"? "Isn't it cold today?"

Women are always cold, I thought, and how did they expect to be anything else, going about as they did with scarcely any clothes on? And did she ever have a bath, I wondered, looking at her bare legs. When I noticed a big

125

toe nail poking out of the end of her mule I hastily averted my gaze.

"You're nice and cozy in here anyway," I said.

"I've not long lighted it," she answered quickly, almost defensively, as though I'd accused her of something. "The lady upstairs lent me a mite of coal."

"What about your visit to Johnny?"

"I saw him Wednesday."

"You said you would phone me at once.

"I was just going to."

"What did he say?"

"He said he'd be sending you a visit soon.

"Yes, yes. What about Evie?"

"Oh, he says he doesn't want her to go away.

"Why ever not?"

"I don't know. It's what he said."

"But he must have given a reason. Did you explain to him properly that it's a kennel and not a friend?"

"Yes, I told him."

"Well, what did he say?"

"He said he'd soon be out to look after her himself."

"Soon!" I exclaimed. "It'll be another five months!"

"Four," said Megan. "That's not so long."

"It may not be long for him," I said angrily. "He's got plenty of four months in his life. But a dog only lives about twelve years. Four months is a large slice out of

Evie's life." Megan knitted her pallid brows at me. "Are you sure you told him everything I asked you to?"

"Yes, I told him."

"I can't understand him. Why on earth should he mind? I wish I'd seen him myself. When is the next visit due?"

"It should be in about two weeks."

"I hope I get it. I'm most anxious to speak to him about her."

"What's the matter with her?" asked Megan.

I opened my mouth. Then I closed it. Then I opened it again.

"Perhaps you didn't catch what I told you on the phone?"

"About her not going out?" said Megan, staring at me with her pale green eyes. I nodded encouragingly. "But I thought you said you'd had her over to Barnes with you?"

"What's that got to do with it?"

"Well, she's *been* out, hasn't she?"

I contemplated her for a moment in silence. Her black hair was coiled above one eye in a sort of limp loop. Was the woman half-witted? Or was she fooling me?

"You think it's enough for a young dog to have a week-end of exercise once in six months?"

"I don't know. I never thought."

"I expect you never thought to tell Johnny about it either?"

"I told him," she replied tonelessly.

"That was good of you," I said with a kind smile, " after they'd asked you not to." She squinted at me in her focusing way. "Millie and Tom," I added.

"They never said nothing."

"Oh come now! Not after you talked it over with them on Easter Sunday?"

"I never said nothing," said she, poking at the fire.

"I'm not blaming you at all, you understand." After a moment I added: "You see Millie says he doesn't know."

"Does she?" Megan fixed her pale eyes on me again.

"Yes. She says Tom told him different. They thought he had enough to worry him already, she said." Megan did not speak. "Wasn't that what they told you when they asked you not to bother him about Evie?"

"They never said nothing to me," she replied flaccidly.

"I feel certain Johnny would have let me put her in a kennel if he'd understood what was happening to her."

"P'raps he didn't know what to think if Tom told him different," supplied Megan helpfully.

"Very likely. What did Tom tell him?"

"I don't know what he told him."

"But you were there too!" I exclaimed irritably.

"I wasn't listening. I don't pay no attention to what Tom says."

"But you *must* have been listening! You said on the

phone that you'd heard Millie ask Johnny about sending Evie to my cousin."

"I never said," said Megan flatly.

"But Megan, you did. I remember distinctly."

"I never."

I looked at her with distaste. Johnny had often told me that she was as obstinate as a mule, and that if she had once adopted a line of argument that suited her, the most incontrovertible proof of error would not induce her to relinquish it. I did not want to antagonize her. Her disdainful references to Tom suggested another tack.

"What do you think of Tom?"

She shrugged:

"He's dry."

"You don't like him?"

"I don't take that notice of him." With a bloodless hand she pinned back the limp loop, which had come unstuck. "He doesn't like me, I know that."

Here, at any rate, was a truth; the first, in all probability, that we had stumbled on.

"He doesn't like me either," I said.

She studied me curiously for a moment.

"Have you been having a row?"

"Well, we've had a few words," I replied carefully, "but it seems to have blown over. I kept Evie a couple of days longer than I said and they made a fuss. In fact they were jolly rude. I was sorry really, because I'm fond of Millie and didn't mean to upset her. Tom was at the back of it all."

"I don't like that Tom," said Megan reflectively, scratching her leg. "He's jealous."

This remark stunned me to such an extent that I gaped at her. Then I recovered myself and said:

"You mean he's jealous of me?" She nodded, with a smirk. "I guessed that. But it's his own fault. If he'd taken the poor bitch out more and thrashed her less she'd have liked him instead of me."

Megan gave a single shrill squeal and clapped her hand over her mouth, as she always did when she laughed to conceal the fact that her front teeth were badly decayed. I looked at her in astonishment.

"He's jealous of Millie too," she said spluttering.

"Is he?" What was so funny about that, I wondered.

"He thinks you're after her," said Megan with another squeak.

I stared at her in stupefaction.

"I? Millie?" I couldn't take it in. "What on earth are you talking about?"

With an effort she pulled herself together.

"You kiss her, don't you? He doesn't like that."

"Nonsense!" I felt my face redden. "I've kissed Millie for years in a friendly way."

"He doesn't like it. You ask Johnny. Johnny told him not to be so daft."

"When did this happen?"

"Oh a long time back. But I thought it'd come up again from something I heard Tom say."

"What did you hear him say?"

Megan hesitated. Then she giggled.

"I heard him say 'I'll knock his block off if I see him do it again!' I don't like that Tom."

"He must be mad!" I said disgustedly. Millie! But now that such a monstrous conjunction had been suggested, I remembered some puzzling incidents. "Well, I suppose it's something to know. Thanks for telling me. I'm surprised that Johnny didn't." The subject was embarrassing, to say the least. My gaze wandered round the bare, untidy room. "If Johnny won't let me put Evie into the country, do you think he'd sell her to me?"

"Sell her?" Megan regarded me attentively. "No, I don't think he'd do that."

"You see he'll never be able to keep her himself. It's out of the question. He'll have to get a job as soon as he's released, and he'll have his work cut out to keep you and the children—four of them," I added, nodding at her stomach, "without the trouble and expense of a large dog. How will he feed her, for instance? She needs horse meat, it's expensive, and Tom has to stand in a queue for it. You can't see Johnny doing that, can you, even if he had the time? And I don't suppose *you're* going to, are you?"

"Oh, *I'm* not!" said Megan with a laugh.

"Well then. And who's to take her out? She's wild. You couldn't possibly hold her, and Johnny will be at work all day."

"I don't think he'll sell her," said Megan.

"I'll give him a good price for her. I'll give him twenty-five pounds." I hadn't thought of the sum; it simply came into my head. Megan goggled at me. "You'd sooner have that than the dog, wouldn't you?"

"Oh, *I* don't want the dog!"

"It's far more than she's worth, I'm sure. The poor thing's no good at all now. And a sum like that would be a great help to you both, wouldn't it? Don't you think it's a sensible plan?"

A pleading note had entered my voice. Megan noticed it.

"Why do you want her if she's no good?"

"I don't want her. That's to say I can't keep her, any more than Johnny can. Just those few days with her reduced me to a nervous wreck. But I'm sorry for her. That's all. I've no other interest. I—I can't bear to think of her. Her loneliness. I can't bear it. It upsets me. But if she belonged to me, you see, I could fix her up somewhere better. . . ."

"I don't think he'll sell her," said Megan. "But I'll ask him if you like. I'll be writing him soon."

"Yes, do. I shall ask him myself when I see him. But I've a feeling it's terribly urgent. Tell him I'll put twenty-five pounds into your hands for him the moment he agrees."

"Oh, I'll tell him, don't worry." And it did seem a message she might possibly get right. "But I don't think he'll sell her. He's soppy about her."

"Soppy?"

"You know, sentimental. Tears run down his cheeks when he speaks of her. They do, honest! It's a scream! He asks after her every time I go, and he only has to say her name and the tears run out of his eyes! Like a baby!"

What *was* the woman talking about? I said:

"But he hasn't seen her since she was a puppy."

"Oh, he thinks the world of her," said Megan with a laugh.

Incomprehensible people! What was one to make of them? I got up to go.

"Well, if he thinks that much of her," I said brusquely, "he'd better sell her to me at once, or she'll be dead by the time he comes out!"

Little Rita was still mincing up and down outside, making her buttocks slide. I scowled at her as I passed. A mistake, as I was to discover to my cost. She stared at me silently with a wide-eyed baffling look she had doubtless learnt to bestow upon detectives and other unwelcome callers. Before turning the corner I glanced back. She was still standing there, her finger in her mouth, gazing after me.

But I could not rest. The image of the frustrated dog continued to haunt me, and the suspicions that had been fretting my mind, now more outraged than ever, were sharpened by my conversation with Megan. Tom Winder hated me. I had sensed it before, now I had no doubt. A number of inexplicable incidents fell convincingly into place around Megan's shocking revelation; and in an atmosphere so much more sinister and highly charged it seemed to me absolutely imperative to expose the truth of the matter at once. What were their intentions with regard to Evie? If I asked for her again, what would the answer be? That, to my troubled mind, was all that counted. That was the test upon which everything else depended. Was it really possible that I should be obstructed? How could I find out, without disturbing the peace which Millie's letter—now in my hand and still unanswered— so disarmingly re-established? Actually there was nothing more I could do for Evie at present. I had only just taken her back, and had not the time, nor, it had to be admitted, the inclination, to have her again. I loved her, but the sweet creature was too much of a good thing; I was not ready for another dose of her yet. Nor did I want to go to Stratford to see her. I wanted to see her, but I did not want to go to Stratford. The very thought of my next visit, still some weeks off, filled me with utter repugnance. Yet although I had no immediate intention or desire to carry her off again, the suspicion engendered in me by this letter and intensified by Megan's disclosure that I should meet with resistance if I tried, affected me like a fever. How could I find out? How could I frame a reply which, without being objectionable, would force them to put their cards on the table? The subject had become so tender that even to mention Evie might seem to them like taking a liberty, like further interference in their stupid lives. . . . Perhaps I thought with savage humor, putting the letter down, it would be wiser to let sleeping dogs lie, and wait until I had seen Johnny or received an answer to my proposition. . . . But wait, wait, wait! Life was nothing but waiting! Waiting for this, waiting for that. . . . Did *they* wait? Not a bit of it! They did as they wished and got what they wanted! Besides—I picked up the letter again—if this soothing peace was genuine how could it be disturbed? With an easy twist of the wrist Millie had set the clock back; my honor had been vindicated, apologies made, she had put herself in the wrong.

Presumably, therefore, the *status quo* was wholly restored—friendship, cash, confidence: confidence, dog. Indeed, why hesitate? This artless acquittal actually dictated its artless reply, the reply of the innocent man. Of course! The trick, if trick it were, was catching! I sat down at once and scribbled off a jolly, even effusive, letter to say how happy hers had made me and how relieved I was that our friendship was unimpaired. I inquired affectionately after everyone's health, said that I was particularly cheerful myself since I was shortly to receive a visit to Johnny, and ended with a deliberate lie: "There's a chance of my getting the loan of a car this coming weekend, in which case I should like to run up to see you all. I might also, with your permission, carry Evie off to Barnes in it, just for one night. It would be a good opportunity to get her out into the country, and this time, you may be sure, I shall be most careful to bring her back on the dot."

Now we shall learn the truth, I thought grimly as I posted it. If the reply was satisfactory I could always say that the car had failed to materialize.

Millie's answer came by return of post.

> Dear Frank,
>
> thank you for the welcome letter which I received quite safe and how pleased I am that you are in such good spirits and will be seeing Johnny soon,

I hope the weather stays fine for you and that you will both have a nice time, Dickie's face is a lot better you will be glad to hear though his cold still trouble him and I am giving him a sirup which I have from the chemist but "rest assured', I will soon have him well again. I shall be at home this Saturday if you care to come but do not come on the Sunday as we are going over to Megan's for the day and I am afraid you will not be able to take Evie out for a while as she is not well.

so cheerio and all the best.

"Not well!" The words struck a chill to my heart. Then I perceived that, in conjunction with "for a while," a natural feminine unwellness was perhaps intended. I had not thought of that. Could it be true? Or was it an excuse? I made inquiries in the dog world. Yes, it could be true and probably was; Evie was about eight months old, the age when bitches usually endure their first heat. She would be beyond my reach for three weeks. How maddening! Now I would have to wait all that time before I could put my doubts to the test again! Yet Millie's letter was unexceptionable, friendly, prompt, even sprightly—and she could afford all that, I thought darkly, with such a magnificent checkmate move.

And then, suddenly, the very next day—Megan was

out in her reckoning, it seemed—the visit to Johnny arrived! I recognized it instantly, the buff official envelope,
and pounced upon it. The slip inside, signed by the
Governor, authorized a visit to the prisoner named for
twenty minutes any afternoon between 1.30 and 3.30.
Johnny! At last! Then I perceived, to my chagrin, that
the prisoner named was not Johnny at all but someone
called Albert Newby. Fools! Dolts! They had sent me
the wrong visit! In a burst of vexation I returned it to
the Governor with a terse note to say that a mistake had
been made, that the prisoner I knew and wished to see
was John Burney, and that I had never heard of Albert
Newby in my life. Could the mistake kindly be rectified
instantly.

But the amended visit was not returned. Nothing
came, no acknowledgment, no reply of any sort. Three
days of fruitless waiting passed and I started to fidget in
my mind. The fourth day brought no news. Nebulous
doubts and fears began to assail me. On the sixth day, in
a state of anxiety bordering on terror, I flew down to
Megan. Hurrying up the steps I rattled the letter-box.
There was no response. I rattled again. And again. How
everything conspired to frustrate me! What should I do?
As I stood there by the closed door, agitated and at a loss,
it seemed to me that the dirty curtains moved slightly.
Was it my imagination? With a desperate ferocity I at-

tacked the letter-box once more. Suddenly a window above my head shot up and a floozie looked out. It was "the lady upstairs," Megan's friend.

"Do you know where Megan is?"

"She's here," said the lady upstairs, and Megan's head popped out too. They were like two hens peering out of a crate.

"I'll be down," said she and, in a moment, opened the door.

"I was afraid you were out," I said. "I've been rattling and rattling."

"Didn't Rita hear you?"

"Yes," I said grimly. "If she's here."

She was, sitting up at the table in the front room, surrounded by colored chalks with which she was busy drawing what looked like an endless row of upright cucumbers in an exercise book. Sprawled over the table, with her tongue out, she took no notice of us at all.

"Didn't you hear the door?" asked Megan perfunctorily as we passed. Without detaching her attention from art, little Rita shook her head, then nodded it, then shook it again. I sat down heavily in Johnny's arm-chair and explained to Megan what had happened, while she studied me with her pale, cold eyes.

"Have I done wrong?" I asked, staring at her appealingly.

139

"What did you want to send it back for?"

"But it was the natural thing to do. I wanted to see Johnny, not Albert Newby."

"I expect you'd have seen him if you'd gone," said she with a faint smile.

"It was a trick, you mean?" The hideous fear had ruined me all night. "But how? How?"

"Oh, *I* don't know," said Megan virtuously. "But there must be plenty of boys there that don't come from London and haven't no one to visit them, and perhaps they sell their visits to the London boys for a cigarette."

"But isn't it frightfully dangerous?"

Megan shrugged contemptuously.

"There's hundreds there, coming and going. The screws never know half their names."

"Then if I'd gone and asked for Newby, Johnny would have appeared?"

"I expect so," said Megan amused. "Of course I don't know."

I groaned with horror. It was so simple, so obvious, as soon as it was explained.

"Why ever didn't he warn me?"

"I expect he thought you'd fluff. Why didn't you just keep the visit instead of sending it back?"

"But it's what I do!" I cried despairingly. "It's what I do! It's the way I think! If things go wrong I set them right.

If memoranda come to my office with mistakes, I point out the mistakes and have them corrected. It's what I do. I'm not used to this kind of thing." Megan was examining me with critical detachment. "I'm afraid I've got him into the most serious trouble," I said humbly.

"He'll have to use his loaf," said she with a laugh. "And Newby too."

"God! What have I done! Will he lose his remission, do you think?"

"I shouldn't worry," she said kindly. "Johnny's smart. I expect he'll think up something." After a pause she added: "Would you like a cup of tea? I was just going to make one?"

I accepted gratefully. She was sorry for me and I was touched. As soon as she left the room I took a pound note out of my pocket and put it quickly on the mantelpiece under the frame in which Dickie and I lived cheek by jowl. Turning round I caught Rita's eye, before she reapplied it to her industrious occupation with art. She was really quite a pretty child, I thought, with her pale, elfin, clever little face, and—the mocking reflection occurred to me—she would not have perpetrated my blunder!

"What are you doing?" I asked respectfully.

"Draw-ring."

"And what are you drawing?"

"You."

I craned my head to look. A sort of turnip had been added to the field of cucumbers. Odious brat! A sudden annoyance took me at having parted with my pound and I gazed at it with a frown. Had she seen me put it there? Could I not get it back? I glanced at her; her head was bent, but I had the feeling that she was watching me. Leaning my elbow on the mantelpiece I gave the distance to the note a swift measuring look; if I lowered my arm . . . But once again, glancing back at Rita, I could have sworn that, in that brief instant, she had peeped up. Abandoning the hopeless attempt, I returned to my chair and stared dejectedly at the carpet. Megan came in with the tea.

"What do you think will happen now?" I asked.

"I don't know. If I don't hear soon I shall apply for another visit on compassionate grounds. They don't like to refuse that."

Could I ask to go with her? I could not.

"Will you let me know as soon as you get news? I shall be worried to death until I hear."

"Yes, I'll phone you. Do you want a cup?" she asked, turning to Rita. Without looking up, the child wagged her head in assent. "Haven't you a tongue in your head?" Megan inquired phlegmatically. Since it was still sticking out, the question was superfluous, and Rita appeared to take it as such for she did not deign to reply. "Johnny's mother gave her those chalks she's playing with. They was over Sunday." She laughed. "Dickie won't have nothing to do with me now. He won't so much as look at me. He peeps at me out of the corner of his eye and if I look he looks away. It's a scream! But most of the time he cried to be taken home. 'Home!' That's what he calls it."

"Did they say anything about Evie? I wanted to take her out, but Millie said she was in heat. It could be true, but I wondered. I keep imagining that I'm being prevented from seeing her."

"Yes, they said she wasn't well." Megan paused, then tittered. "I don't think you'll get hold of her again."

"What do you mean by that?" I asked sharply.

"It was something Tom said."

"What did he say?"

"He said about not letting her go."

"He said what! How did the matter come up?"

Megan eyed me with amusement.

"I said you wanted to buy her. Was that all right?"

"Of course. Why not? She's not their dog. What exactly did Tom say?"

She knitted her anemic brows:

"He said 'The dog doesn't leave my house again.'"

"I'll put the R.S.P.C.A. on to him!" I cried. Then, with an effort, I brought it out: "Look, I *must* see Johnny. If you get a visit to him first I would like to go with you. Do you mind?"

"Oh, I don't mind."

"Then you'll let me know the moment you hear anything?"

"Yes, I'll phone you."

And how time dragged! The rest of that upsetting day passed, the next and the next. When I returned home in the evenings from work I dared not leave my telephone in case Megan rang, yet I could not concentrate my attention on anything indoors. What dire consequence of my stupidity had befallen Johnny? Deprivation of privilege, loss of remission, solitary confinement, bread-and-water: my mind, a prey to every kind of hideous imagining, however improbable, was ceaselessly engaged with his inevitable punishment. And in my dreams I saw him thrashed, the belt taken off, the lash laid on his honey-colored flesh. To have exposed his deception to the Governor himself! If I had actually designed to in-jure him—and the knowledge that I had, in fact, been angry with him shattered me the more—I could not have put him more successfully on the spot. At length, after four days of the utmost wretchedness, I could bear it no longer and hurried over to Megan's, but rattle at the door as I might no one came. On the following day I went again, with the same result, and as I stood there drumming upon the shut house, which might or might not be empty but which vouchsafed no response, a feeling of total despair overcame me, of the loneli-ness of life, the impossibility of human communication, the futility of all endeavor. Knock, knock as one might against the heart of man, it gave forth only a hollow mockery of sound.

Putting up my jacket collar, for a drizzle of rain had started to fall, I turned away.

Megan and little Rita were coming down the street towards me! Rushing to meet them I cried:

"Is there any news?"

"Yes, I've just seen him. I was going to phone you."

"You've seen him! How is he? What happened?"

"Oh, he's all right," said she with a smile.

The relief was almost more than I could bear.

"He didn't get into trouble?"

"Well, the Governor sent for him, but he managed to scrape out of it."

"What a mercy! He wasn't punished at all, then?" She shook her head, amused. "Was he angry with me?"

"Well, he was a bit browned off and he asked why you'd sent the visit back, but I told him what you'd said and that you was upset, and he said to give you his best and tell you not to worry."

I could almost have kissed her. Then I noticed her appearance. She was all dolled up, her face thick with slap. She was wearing a two-piece costume, a black tunic, and light gray skirt, so unsuitable to her compassionate grounds that she could only have put it on purposely, to accentuate them. Neither garment, indeed, could any longer contain her swollen stomach; safety pins secured them where they failed to meet. Over her head was draped a scarf with "Into Battle" printed round its borders; tanks, planes, and soldiers crawled on her black hair, and the long barrel of a howitzer pointed down her forehead into her left eye.

I said coldly:

"Why did you not phone me when the visit came?"

"I did phone you. There was no reply."

"When did you phone?"

"Yesterday."

"At what time?"

She hesitated:

"It must have been about six."

That was the time when I had been rattling at her door. I stared at her. The nearest public telephone, the one they generally used, was just round the corner in the Fulham Palace Road. I had passed it on my way to visit her. Could she have been actually in it as I went by? Or had she rung up from some other box? Or was it simply a lucky shot?

Or, darker suspicion still, had she been lurking all the time in the silent house, knowing who knocked and bent upon not sharing the visit in her pocket? I stared at her steadfastly. If my eyes could have torn her open she would have fallen apart at my feet.

"When did the visit come?"

"Yesterday morning."

"You must have applied for it directly after I saw you?"

"I didn't apply. I was just going to when it came. It was the official visit."

The official visit! I had forgotten all about it! And it had gone, of course, to her, not to me. It struck me then, with the force of a blow, that I had been conceded nothing after all. The visit I had had and bungled had not been an official one, Megan had not stood aside for me, nothing had been given up. I might do what I could for them, nothing would be done for me. Like the letter I had received and ignored, the visit had been something extra, something squeezed in, something that could be spared without loss to themselves, a sop, a fob. . . .

"Did you ask him about Evie?"

"Yes, he won't sell her. I thought he wouldn't."

"You told him the price I named?"

"Yes, I told him. He wouldn't hear of it. He—" She suddenly spluttered, clapping her hand to her mouth. Of course! Of course! How could I have been so naïve? Was it likely that Johnny in prison would allow me to hand twenty-five pounds to his wife to "keep" for him till he came out? A fine joke he must have thought it!

"Are you coming in?" Megan asked, looking up at the weeping sky. I mumbled an excuse and left her.

Dear Millie,

I expect Megan will have told you by now about my misfortune over the visit to Johnny. It was sent in the name of some other prisoner, and I thought this a mistake and returned it for correction. But it was a trick of Johnny's and if I'd gone I would have seen him. I was terribly worried because I thought I'd got him into trouble, but luckily he managed to get out of it. It has been a great disappointment to me too. I'm afraid I shan't be able to come up and see you this weekend, but could I come the following Wednesday, when I'm beginning a week's holiday? I'm going down into the country afterwards and would like to take Evie with me if I may. She will be over her indisposition by then and it will be good for her. I would bring her back to you the weekend after. I hope you are all quite well and that Dickie's health has ceased to be an anxiety to you.

I brooded over this letter one evening a few days later. It seemed a perfectly good letter, easy, frank, friendly, well-intentioned. By pretending ignorance of Tom's remark—and they could hardly suppose that Megan had repeated it to me—it would discover what weight, if any, was to be attached to it. And everything depended upon that. No dog, no money! I said to myself. The date of the proposed visit had been carefully selected. Evie would be completely off heat by then, so that excuse could not be used again, and Millie's half-day would avoid a meeting with Tom. I dreaded seeing him. The acutest embarrassment overcame me at the thought of meeting either of them, but him I dreaded. How he must have chuckled at the failure of my mission to Johnny! Then the proposition itself was close to the truth. I had made no actual plans for a holiday, but I was terribly run down, I longed to get away and had now a quite urgent desire to see Evie again and to take her with me.... The only thing was, ought I not, perhaps, to put Dickie's keep into the envelope too? No, why should I? No dog, no money! Yet, on the other hand, it was what I had always done in the past when I had had to postpone my monthly visit; it would be the normal thing to do, and I wanted everything to seem normal.... I brooded. To withhold the money; that would probably look to them what in fact it would be, blackmail, threat. Might it not put their backs up?

And surely it should be my policy to give them every pretext for generosity. . . . I brooded somberly. Then I put the money in. For Evie's sake, I said. But it was more than that, I knew; it was a propitiatory sacrifice, for the truth of the matter was that I was scared stiff.

> Dear Frank,
>
> thank you for your welcome letter and for Dickie's keep all of which I received safe and for which I thank you, I was sorry to hear of the loss of your visit. I do not think I would have known either what to do if I had received a visit like that in a wrong name, but "all's well that ends well" and "who knows" but that you may have the luck of another visit sooner than you think seeing that Megan will not be able to go much longer, I will be at home Wednesday if you would care to come but Johnny has wrote me that Evie is not to be taken out of this house until he comes to fetch her himself so I don't think you will be able to take her, and perhaps its as well seeing she is so tiresome at times. The weather is more settled now isn't it, it looks as though summer has come at last.

So here it was!

Dear Millie,

I'm sorry, but I really must have an explanation of your letter. Am I to understand that I am no longer allowed to take Evie out at all? If that is what Johnny is now saying, then he has changed his mind, for not long ago he wished me to take her as you know. If I am now forbidden to take her there must be a reason for it, and I must know the reason. It sounds as though I am no longer trusted. Am I no longer trusted? Your letter makes me very uncomfortable.

Dear Frank,

I cannot for the life of me understand, why it is that you, all of a sudden, have taken such an interest in Evie, and I would not like to be bad friends with you or you to take any offense with this letter, but I must say that the sooner you lose that interest, the better our friendship will be. In fact I don't see what it has to do with you, as Tom and I keep and feed her and she gets taken out now of an evening, and as she was left in my care I am responsible for her.

As soon as I received this letter I flew down to Megan. Little Rita and her terrible twin-sister Gwen, weekending from Cardiff, were sitting on the steps in the sunshine whispering together over some pebbles they had laid out between them. Absorbed in their sorcery they did not look up. Megan opened the door.

"You were quite right!" I exclaimed, as I followed her into the front room. "They won't let me take Evie out *at all* now!" I flourished the letters in her face. "Not *at all*! Millie says that Johnny's written her to say that neither I nor anyone else may take her out of the house until he fetches her himself. I don't believe a word of it! He never said such a thing, did he?"

"I don't know," said Megan, gaping at me.

"You don't know! You must know! Did he ever say such a thing to you?"

"He never said it to me, but he might have said it to them."

"But why? Why? What for?"

"So as not to upset them, perhaps," said Megan dimly.

"Upset them!" I shouted. "All this bosh about not upsetting people! *He's* not to be upset! *They're* not to be upset! The only one who doesn't matter is the poor bloody dog! What happens to her is of no consequence, I suppose?" Megan goggled at me. "But I don't believe it! I don't believe Johnny ever said such a thing! I don't believe they had a letter from him at all!"

"Yes, they had a letter, because they told me so when I was up there last Sunday. But they never showed it me."

I glared at her.

"You were up there! What did they say?"

"They never said nothing."

"They must have said something."

"No, they never said nothing."

"Don't be ridiculous! Did you all sit there like mutes?"

"They never said nothing," Megan chanted.

"Do you mean the subject never came up at all? Not even about Johnny's refusal to sell her?"

"No, they never said nothing so I never said nothing."

My head was spinning round.

"Did you see Evie?"

"Yes, I saw her."

My voice broke a little as I asked:

"How was she?"

"She was all right."

"And nothing was said about her or me at all?"

"No."

I gave it up.

"Look here," I said. "When are you going to see Johnny again?"

"It'll be about a fortnight before the next visit comes."

"Can't you ask for an earlier one on compassionate grounds? I want to go with you."

"I've just had one. They wouldn't give me another so soon."

I stared at her.

"Do you mean you've been *again* since I last saw you?"

"Yes, I went yesterday."

"I see." Beyond her shoulder, through a gap in the rep curtains, the two children were visible crouched together like witches over their pebbles on the sunlit doorstep. I brought my terrified gaze back to her with an effort. "Well, I must really ask to go with you on the next official visit. It's essential for me to see Johnny now."

"They said they was coming next time."

"The beasts!"

Megan studied me silently. Then she said:

"What does it all matter? It's only a dog."

For a moment I gazed at her speechlessly.

"Even a dog has a right to its life."

"There are more important things to think about."

She meant, presumably, the infant forming in her belly. I picked up my hat and walked out of the house without another word.

It was the loveliest spring. Day after day dawned the serenest, sweetest unclouded blue, and going to and from my work I thought constantly of Evie shut up in the Winders' back yard. Indeed, I thought of nothing else; it weighed upon my heart like some settled sorrow, and the very beauty of the weather, this springing time of the year, wrung me the more. I recalled her bright face, so eager and so gay, with the flying bird on its forehead, and the communicative looks she had fastened upon me. I remembered the strange game she had played with me in my flat and, with a pang, the last I had seen of her as she slunk, in that abject way, into the Winders' scullery. That she had relied upon me I felt sure. That she was awaiting my return I had no doubt at all. I knew that she loved me and listened for me, that whenever a knock came at the door her tall, shell-like ears strained forward with the hope "Is it he?" Impotent rages shook me, and my mind was ceaselessly engaged in retracing the steps that had led to this impasse and seeking ways of recovery or revenge. How deeply I now regretted having sent Millie her month's money! Well, she would get no more and we would see then where the shoe pinched! On the other hand I also regretted not having sent Johnny that five pounds he had wanted weeks ago for his tobacco; if it had opened up communication between us it might have been worth while, for I still found it hard to believe that he really understood what was going on, or that, if I had managed to tell him myself, I should have failed to convince him. Could I not get at him somehow with my version of the story? Books seemed to reach him; what if I sent him one and slipped a letter in? Even if it fell into official hands it could not matter. . . . I did this and, copying out the letter, posted it to him separately also as another of those unofficial communications that might or might not get through. And the beautiful days slid silently by. . . . How could I get even with Tom? Why not put the R.S.P.C.A. on to him, as I had threatened to do? He would not like that! I hovered indecisively over the telephone for some days; then I rang the Society and spoke to an Inspector. I explained the circumstances of the case and asked if there were grounds for interference. Certainly, said he; what was the name and address? But I did not give it. I knew I could not. I told myself that to draw official attention to Evie might do her more harm than good; but the truth was that I feared that nothing of whatever I hoped for from Johnny's promises for the future could survive such an act. Nevertheless it was with a feeling of consolation that I put the receiver down, as though I had taken upon life itself a subtle revenge.

And then the most delightful idea occurred to me, and my imagination played happily with it for some days. I would steal the dog! It was perfectly easy. They were all going off to see Johnny on the next visit; Evie would be alone in the house. What sweeter time to take her from

them than when they were enjoying the happiness denied
to me! There was that unused, dustbin-cluttered path-
way at the back, the flimsy wooden gate ... When dusk
fell—for they always made a day of such expeditions and
would certainly repair to Megan's for tea on the way
home—I could slip in unobserved. Evie would not bark,
she would know who it was and fly silently into my
arms. What gladness! What delight! Even if she were
in the house, the scullery door-latch would present no
difficulty. Then I would loosen and move a stake in the
fence to make it appear that the imprisoned animal had
broken out and away at last. Returning from their selfish
pleasures and their schemings against me they would
find her gone! And they could never know. They
would suspect, but they could prove nothing. I would
stow her away somewhere in the country and visit
her—aye, visit *her* at any rate!—whenever I liked....
Or join Johnny in Wormwood Scrubs, my imagination
added, which would surely be to gain my ends in another
way, for it would give me that access to him that I had
so long lost, so long desired. This thought afforded me
a certain ironic amusement and, recollecting my indignation over his remark about my cousin, I reflected that
there wasn't, after all, much to choose between us; he
was a crook in fact and I was a crook at heart: in my case
the courage was wanting....

Thereafter, amid these shifting images of love and hatred, a kind of lassitude fell upon me. I forced myself away on a week's holiday and derived benefit from it. I began to forget. The thought of Evie troubled me less and less, was more easily shrugged off; the obligation under which, it seemed to me, she had put me lost its strength. May passed, June got under way; I thought of her now scarcely at all, only when distasteful reminders called up the fading grief. Millie wrote from time to time, at first with a naïve pretense that my unresponsiveness—for I answered nothing—was accidental; then with an equally naïve request for explanation; then with reproaches for once again breaking my promises. The shoe pinches! I thought callously. Towards the end of June she capitulated; since she could no longer afford to keep Dickie she would have to give in ("how you will laugh") and let me have Evie after all ("but I hope that this time you will keep your word and return her at the end of a week"). I had won. But I no longer wanted my victory. I no longer wanted the dog. I no longer wanted anything. The letter was easily found fault with: "Still bargaining with me . . . still suggesting that I don't know how to behave . . . she'll have to send Dickie back now and serve her right . . . it'll be parting with Johnny for the second time . . . perhaps she'll understand now what parting with him meant to me. . . ." Later on the "lady upstairs" phoned to say that

Megan was going into hospital. She could have gone into the morgue for all I cared. And then I received an official visit to Johnny. Megan's pupping, I thought. He can spare me a moment now. I won't go! But I did.

It was a curious thing, but the moment his neat, light figure came into the room where we were all waiting, I experienced again the sensation which the sight of him managed so often to convey, of being somehow or other at fault. As I watched him standing there, searching about with his beautiful eyes, and tasted silently, though for no more than a few beats of the pulse, the happiness of being singled out by him; as I waited quietly until the eyes found their mark, and the light of recognition sprang, and the lips moved in a slight intimate smile, and then there he was, bearing down upon me with his springing gait, I felt strangely abashed and confused, so that long though I had sought and planned for this interview, I found myself with nothing whatever to say, only:

"Johnny."

He sat down opposite me at the end of the long table.

" 'Ow 'ave you been keeping, Frank?"

"All right. And you?"

He made a grimace.

"Browned off! I'm well in meself though." Then, almost at once:

"'Ave you seen 'er lately, Frank?"

In the momentary doubt that this question posed, I recollected the confusion over identities that had occurred during our interview in the police station cell; but looking now at his rather pale and puffy face with the shadows beneath the eyes, I understood to whom he referred and that I had failed in a duty.

"No, Johnny, I haven't."

"I just wondered. I've 'ad a letter from 'er, but not for three days."

"How was she?"

"Oh, she was doing well, she said. It was another boy, you know. They say 'e's smashing, the nurses and that. She's going to 'ave 'is photo took as soon as she can and send it to me. I mean to 'ave 'im christened 'Frank'."

"Oh thank you, Johnny. That'll be fine." He began to gnaw at his thumb. He had very well-shaped hands, slender yet strong, and I noticed that the nails, which he had always tended to bite, had been eaten down to the quicks. "I'm sorry, Johnny. It was careless of me. I ought to have asked after her before I came. I didn't think."

"It don't matter. Only I was expecting another letter and—you know 'ow it is—you get thinking in a cowson of a place like this."

"It must have been a worry for you, being shut up at such a time."

"I done me nut. I applied for permission to go and see 'er, and you'd think they'd grant you a thing like that, now wouldn't you? But, ah they'd shit 'emselves, the bastards, before they'd do anything for you!" His face was improved by the flush of this momentary choler. Megan had been granted extra visits whenever she'd asked for them; "they" did not seem to me to have behaved too badly; but I did not say so, for I did not wish to talk about Megan.

"I expect she's all right," I said easily.

"I expect so."

I smiled at him.

"Well, here we are at last, Johnny. I'm pleased to see you."

"I'm pleased to see you too, Frank." The response was instant and warm. "And I'm sorry not to 'ave seen you before. It wasn't that I didn't think of you, because I did. I've thought of you a lot in 'ere and all what you've done for me. But I 'ad to try to please everyone and I couldn't do no more than that. I done me best."

I nodded. He was perfectly sincere, and sitting there, face to face with him, I had no desire at all, when the words fell between us, to pick any of them up. He had had his shots at me; what did it matter whether they came from the right hand or the left? I could not even remember clearly now what it was that had upset me so much, and I had an uncomfortable feeling—the sight of him conveyed it—that there was something in all this that I had missed, other realities besides my own. Now that I was with him at last, I found it difficult, even distasteful, to recall what my own reality had been.

"I'm afraid I let you down badly over that other visit."

"It don't matter."

"You must have been wild with me."

"Well, I was a bit mad at first. I thought you'd understand, see? But I've forgot about it now."

"Was it very awkward?"

He grinned.

"Well, it took us by surprise, if you know what I mean. When the Governor sent for us we knew we was in for something, but we didn't know what. I thought of a lot of things, but I never thought of that. It come back on us too quick, see? That's where it was."

"Yes, I fairly shot it back, I'm afraid."

"You did an' all!" said Johnny.

"You must have thought me a proper bloody fool."

"That's all right," said he kindly. "You wasn't to know. I saw that afterwards. Where it is, you're always on the fiddle in 'ere, and after a bit you see everything like that, as a fiddle, and so you get to think that everyone else must see things the same way as you do." I nodded. Then I nodded more vigorously. It was, indeed, a profound truth, and the very one that had been troubling my own mind. "I wouldn't 'ave minded for meself, but there was me mate too. You see 'e never wanted to sell me the visit, 'e was windy, but I swore it was safe and that nothing could 'appen—well, I didn't think nothing could. So it looked bad for me, like as if I'd grassed 'im."

"Yes, I see. Did he get into trouble?"

"No, but 'e didn't 'alf piss 'isself."

"How did you get out of it?"

"It was me luck. I said the first thing what come into me nut and it turned out good."

"And what came into your nut?" I asked smiling.

"Oh, I said I was sorry for 'im 'avin' no one to visit 'im, so I give 'im your name and address on the chance you'd come."

"And what did the Governor say?"

" 'E arst 'oo you was, and I said you was a good-'earted old geezer as took an interest in charity and 'elping people. I said you was known to me relatives and was always gaspin' to do something for me."

"And he swallowed that?" Indeed, I thought, looking at his charming, open, boyish face, who could have helped it—or at any rate have failed to welcome a reasonable excuse to probe no further?

"Well, 'e didn't like it, but 'e couldn't do nothing else, could 'e? After all, it might 'ave been."

"Why, yes," I said thoughtfully. "It already covers a number of facts."

A momentary silence fell between us.

" 'Ave you seen Mum lately, Frank?"

"I'm afraid we've fallen out, Johnny."

"Yes, I was sorry to 'ear that. She told me last time she come."

"What did she say?" I asked incuriously.

"About you keeping Evie longer than you said and 'er flyin' off the 'andle."

"Well, that covers a few facts too," I remarked with a smile.

"Where it is," said he gently, "you made things a bit awkward for 'er, see? She 'as to live with Tom and you made things a bit awkward. That's where it is."

I nodded.

"I expect so." I didn't want to go back into it. "I never meant to upset her, Johnny, but. . . . You didn't get any letters from me, I suppose? I wrote two or three, long ones."

"No, Frank, I never 'ad no letters from you."

"I stuck one inside a book not long ago. You didn't get that either? *Bulldog Drummond* the book was called."

"No, I never 'ad nothing from you."

"They were all the same letter anyway, so someone must have got bored reading them, if they were read at all."

"What was they about?"

But no, no! I couldn't bear to go back into it all!

"Johnny," I said earnestly, "are things going to be all right between us now?"

"Of course they are," he replied smiling.

"As it was before?"

"I said so, didn't I?"

"Johnny, I'm frightened."

"Don't be silly." My eyes fell. "Was your letters about Evie?"

My hands began to tremble and I clasped them between my knees.

"I've been trying to tell you about her for months."

"What about 'er?"

I tried to focus.

"About her not going out." It sounded awfully lame.

"Tom said 'e took 'er."

"He didn't, Johnny," I said wearily. "It was a lie. No one took her but I. She was a prisoner like you. Didn't Megan tell you? I asked her to."

"She said you 'ad 'er over to Barnes and was worried about 'er."

"Ah, then you did know."

165

"But what could *I* do? I couldn't do nothing in 'ere."

"Couldn't you have let me send her into the country, like I asked?" I said dully.

" 'Ow could I? It wouldn't 'ave been fair on them. Perhaps it was a mistake to put 'er there in the first place, only I didn't know what else to do with 'er. But I couldn't take 'er away from them again after they'd 'ad the trouble of 'er and got fond of 'er, now could I?"

"Millie always said she was such a nuisance," I murmured.

"That's only Mum's way of talking. She didn't mind. She likes 'aving 'er there, and so does Tom. 'E thinks the world of 'er."

Was it the phrase? Was it the phrase? At any rate I suddenly saw her, clear as crystal, bright as dawn, her strange eyes fixed intently upon me.

"He thrashed her and never took her out!" I cried aloud. "Was that fair on the dog?"

Johnny looked down at his hands, which were resting on the table.

"I told 'im not to 'it 'er," he mumbled in a low thick voice. When he raised his eyes again they were brimming with tears.

"Well, he did hit her!" I said brutally. "He took off his belt to her, the swine! And although she begged him to take her out, he was too bloody lazy!"

" 'E ain't been 'isself lately, that's where it is. 'E gets a bit irritating at times. That trouble 'e 'as with 'is back passage, Mum says the doctors say now it's bad, it's a growth."

"Don't!" I said angrily. To have my hatred of Tom so unfairly undermined was too much.

"Mum says Evie's all right," said Johnny, glaring at me through his tears.

"Is she?" I said more gently. "I find it hard to believe, but I don't know."

" 'Aven't you seen 'er lately, Frank?"

"No, they wouldn't let me. They said you didn't want me to. Oh, Johnny, you never said that, did you?"

"No, Frank." Then he added mildly: "They didn't like what you said about the R.S.P.C.A."

Scandalized I exclaimed: "Megan must have told them!"

"No, it was Rita come out with it."

"Ah, Rita!" I said, with a bitter laugh. "I might have known!" So something *had* been said up at Millie's after all, in spite of Megan's denials. I reflected for a moment. "I'm sorry, Johnny. I'm afraid I've been tactless over all this and made things worse for you than they were. But your dog was so pretty and so lonely."

"Did Mum write you? I told 'er to and to say you was to 'ave Evie for your 'oliday."

I smiled at him.

"I'm keeping the rest of that for you now, Johnny. Do you remember what you said?"

"Of course I do."

"Does it still hold good?"

"Of course it does," he said laughing. "I promised, didn't I? Did Mum write you?"

"Yes, she did, Johnny. I'm afraid I didn't answer." After a moment I added: "The good-hearted old geezer was a bit browned off."

"Now, now, you don't want to take no notice of that. I didn't mean nothing by that. You can 'ave Evie for your 'oliday if you like, Frank, so long as you bring 'er back at the end of it."

"Thank you, Johnny. What are you going to do with her when you come out?"

"I shall fetch 'er 'ome to mine. It'll be the first thing I do."

"Oh do! Oh do!" I said earnestly. "Don't leave her there a second longer than you can help!"

"Of course I'll 'ave to let them 'ave 'er back from time to time."

"You'll send her back to that yard!" I cried aghast.

But he was equally vehement:

"'Ow can I 'elp it? I can't do nothing else. You don't understand. It's the same with Dickie. I can't just go and take 'im away from them. They're struck on 'im now, and

Megan says 'e thinks more of Mum than 'e do of 'er. So what can *I* do? I don't *want* them to 'ave 'im, any more than I want them to 'ave Evie. I want me family and me dog with me. But I can't take everything away from Mum as soon as I come out and leave 'er with nothing, now can I? They don't 'ave much in their lives and they've been good to me while I've been inside. I'll 'ave to be fair to them."

"Leave the child and take the dog," I said gravely. "The child wants to stay, the dog doesn't."

"I'll 'ave to see," he muttered, gnawing his nails.

"Where did you get her, by the way?"

"I bought 'er," said Johnny with a grin. "It was the first thing I done when I'd made a bit of money screwin'. Of course I didn't tell *them* that, for they knew I didn't 'ave the cash, so I said she was give me."

"Why did you buy her?"

He looked at me in surprise.

"I wanted 'er. I saw 'er in a shop winder, and I meant to 'ave 'er. I put down a deposit on 'er, and then I screwed the first 'ouse to get the rest. I'm mad on them dogs, didn't you know? I 'ad one when I was a kid. Didn't Mum tell you? I thought the world of 'er, I did. 'Er name was Evie too. I done me nut when she died. She 'ad some thing went wrong with 'er insides. Oh, I done me nut! You ask Mum. I wouldn't eat. I never ate for days. Oh, I went mad! Mum'll tell you."

I nodded, looking at his flushed face, flushed with the sentimentality of self-dramatization. Then I connected.

"Was that why you asked me for a loan, then? To buy this Evie?"

He shot me a brief glance, sharp, amused.

"Well, she come in."

"And how much did she cost?"

"I give fifteen quid for 'er. She's good, she is. I mean to breed from 'er when I get out." Then he added: "Megan told me you wanted to buy 'er, Frank. But I wouldn't sell 'er. I've thought of 'er every day since I've been in 'ere. Every day! I wouldn't sell 'er to no one, not for nothing. I wouldn't sell 'er for a thousand pounds!"

"That's all right, Johnny. I wasn't going to ask again. But you'll never be able to keep her. You've no idea. She's a wild beast."

"I'll manage some'ow. Would you like 'er for your 'oliday, Frank? Shall I tell Mum to write you again?"

I shook my head.

"Bring her to see me when you come out."

"All right. I'll bring 'er along as soon as I've got 'er. And I'll stay with you the 'ole day. That's a promise."

A bell rang for us to go.

"'Ave you got my fags on you?" he asked in a rapid, urgent whisper.

"Don't be silly, Johnny! It's too dangerous!"

"Come on!" said he, turning on all his charm like a light. "They won't take no notice."

His eyes, tearful a moment ago, were now fairly dancing.

"Johnny, I can't!" A notice on the wall forbade visitors under penalty of prosecution to pass anything to the prisoners, and a large screw—Millie's perhaps—was standing almost at my elbow. Johnny observed the furtive glance I cast at him.

"That's all right. I know 'im. 'E's cushy."

"Anyway I've only Turkish."

"Christ!" said Johnny with disgust. "Never mind. They'll 'ave to do."

I fumbled in my pocket and, coughing and sweating in an excitement which, I afterwards thought when the recollection of it amused me, was probably no less pleasurable than his own, I passed my packet under the table. Johnny's slender hand closed firmly and unfumblingly upon it.

This interview, when the emotional pleasure of seeing Johnny had worn off, left me feeling unaccountably tired and flat, and as my thoughts, in the succeeding days, reverted to it and wandered dully among its shoals and shallows, I found myself afflicted by a despondency which had nothing to do with the perception that I had been put, to a large extent, in the wrong. Say what one might against these people, their foolish frames could not bear the weight of iniquity I had piled upon them; they were, in fact, perfectly ordinary people behaving in a perfectly ordinary way, and practically all the information they had given me about themselves and each other had been true, had been real, and not romance, or prevarication, or the senseless antics of some incomprehensible insect, which were the alternating lights in which, since it had not happened to suit me, I had preferred to regard it. They simply had not wished to worry Johnny, and, it was plain enough, he had had much to worry him already; he had cared about the fate of his dismal wife and family, as Millie had cared about Dickie, and, for all I knew, Tom about Evie; the tears Johnny had shed over his dog had been real tears and, there was no doubt of it, he had terribly missed his smokes. Their problems, in short, had been real problems, and the worlds they so frequently said they thought of each other apparently seemed less flimsy to them than they had appeared to me when I tried to sweep them all away. It was difficult to escape the conclusion, indeed, that, on the whole, I had been a tiresome and troublesome fellow who, for one reason or another, had acted in a manner so intemperate that he might truly be said to have lost his head; but if this sober reflection had upon me any effect at all, it produced no feeling that could remotely be called repentance, but only a kind of listlessness as though some prop that had supported me hitherto had been withdrawn. Yet Johnny had been perfectly nice; what better proof of his affection could I have than the thought that had come to him in the solitude of his cell of calling his new child by my name? And I could have his dog. And soon I should have him. . . . Indeed, I had everything, except the sense of richness, and when the phrase "I 'ad to do me best to please everyone" recurred to my mind, I wondered why so admirable a sentiment made me feel so cross. Beneath such a general smear of mild good nature, I asked myself, could any true values survive? Where everything mattered nothing mattered, and I recollected that it had passed through my mind while I spoke to him that if the eyes that looked into mine took me in at all, they seemed to take me for granted.

Soon afterwards, into my now almost somnambulistic life, a letter from Millie came, an abject, begging letter. Since she had been unable to keep Dickie he had had to be returned to his mother who was now out of hospital; but the child was terribly unhappy, he did nothing but cry all day and would not eat, would I be so kind as to help her? The letter moved and shamed me; I should not have reduced her to that. Poor Millie; I had no desire to see her again, but she was a good creature and I had made her a promise. How could I expect other people to keep their promises to me if I did not keep my own? I sent her a friendly note and enough money to cover the arrears and take her up to the day of Johnny's release. Besides, I reflected, was I not perhaps doing something for Evie too, for if the Winders were able to retain the child it might be easier for Johnny to abstract his dog.

And then, weeks later, he himself phoned, wildly elated; he was just out, was off to fetch Evie at once and would be over to see me soon. Instantly, with the sound of his voice, the exhaustion, apathy almost, that had clogged my spirits for so long, vanished and the old nervous, anxious excitement took its place. Johnny! Johnny and Evie! "Soon" dragged itself out to a week, and how I managed passively to wait I do not know, but I had, after all, been receiving lessons in patience, and wait I did. Then he rang again; it was a Friday evening. "I'll be bringing Evie over tomorrow, Frank. Be with you at two. Okay?"

I had always in the past made elaborate preparations, frequently wasted, for his reception; now I made elaborate preparations for them both. Besides the drink and food, and the present of money I knew he would be glad of, which I gathered together for him, I set the flat lovingly for her as well. Her bowl, her ball, her biscuits, her blanket, everything was put back as it had been before; I stood for two hours in a queue to procure her a succulent piece of horsemeat, and I stocked the vegetable basket with all manner of vegetables for which I had no personal use. And when the time of their arrival drew near, I went out on to my verandah so that I might steal from Time the extra happiness of watching them approach. I knew that he would walk her and the way that he would come, down the towing-path and along The Terrace, and since this stretched below me in all its length, curving away, as the river curved, as far as the eye could reach, I should be able to see them at a considerable distance making, from their respective prisons, their returning way into my life. If Johnny came at all he was always late, and today was no exception; half-past two struck, and "Not this day," I said aloud, as though someone stood beside me under the great arch of the sky. "Take all my other days, but not this one." And then, suddenly, there they were, emerging from among the trees and elder bushes of the towing-path, tiny like figures seen through the wrong end of a telescope, Johnny and Evie, or rather Evie and Johnny, for before they reached the end of the path where it turns into road, I saw him bend and attach her to her lead, and then she came as I remembered her, the pretty sable-gray sprawling bitch, spurning the ground and dragging after her the sturdy, backward-bent figure of her master. With bated breath I watched them approach, growing larger and larger, until they were almost beneath me: and

Johnny never looked up. How strange, I thought as I gazed down at them, drawing them towards me with my eyes, that he did not look up. "Ah, Johnny, look up!" I murmured, but he did not look up, and I recollected then that he never looked back at parting either; it was as though I existed for him only at the point of contact. But if there was nothing in *his* bearing to suggest that the particular direction in which he was moving had for him more interest than any other, Evie, to whom my gaze shifted, gave another impression. And "She remembers!" I said to myself. "I'm sure she remembers!" They reached the entrance to the flats. Craning over the balustrade I watched them arrive. "Now!" I whispered. "Now!" and she turned into the doorway without hesitation, pulling Johnny in after her.

I hurried out to await them on the landing. Johnny made no attempt to use the lift; I heard them plodding and scuffling up the four flights of stairs.

"Evie! Evie!" I cried, and either he released her or she tore herself out of his grasp, for she came bounding up towards me trailing her lead.

If it was true, as Millie had once touchingly suggested, that Evie, in the first instance, had mistaken me for Johnny, it did not look as though she had afterwards mistaken him for me. There seemed no confusion in her mind now, and if the joy with which she greeted me

176

lacked something of the wild abandonment of her Easter welcome, that was no doubt due, I thought, to the fact that here, upon my ground, her enthusiasm was less concentrated, more dispersed; there was my flat as well as myself with which to renew acquaintance. Into this, after she had kissed me, she hurried, re-entering all its rooms and finding again the toys and paraphernalia she had had before; when Johnny and I followed her into the sitting-room she was already in occupation of what she used to regard as her arm-chair, as though she had never left it.

It was the most enchanting, if imperfect, day; it contained all the ingredients, desirable and undesirable, that had long been part and parcel of my friendship with this boy. He was excited, he was affectionate, he was gay; he behaved not merely as though there were something he couldn't sufficiently thank me for, but as though there were something he could never quite make up; he was so much the same as he had been in the beginning, when he and I were all that counted, that the difference, when it appeared, that what he was now doing was simply and still his "best to please everyone," hardly seemed to tell. For he soon declared that he could not stay as long as he had hoped, not more than three hours, Megan was unwell, she had been poorly since her confinement and had come over dizzy, he explained, not meeting my eye; but he would make up for it by bringing Evie again very soon, that was a promise; and then, of course, there were the allusions to financial difficulties which I had foreseen and provided for, and which I now welcomed as I must welcome anything that could help to bind him to me. But the four hours—I managed to extend them to four—that he spent with me were so delightful that they made up, it seemed, for all the frustrations and sorrows of the past—and whatever frustrations and sorrows were to come.

Over our reunion Evie had, at first, the air of presiding. Reclined in her chair, she fixed her gaze intently upon us, observing all we did, as though weighing us up, taking us in. But what she had to take in was, after all, something she had never seen before, the two of us close together, and it may be that this strange sight imposed upon her earlier confidence in our separateness a certain strain. At any rate she soon began to exhibit signs of anxiety. Her face would take on a puzzled, an almost deprecating, look, she would heave a sigh, long and quavering, and, leaving her chair, approach us as if for a nearer view. Sniffing us over, she would rise up to stare into our faces, and sometimes plant a paw upon our breasts, first upon one, then upon the other, as though to say "You and you."

With a strength of purpose remarkable in so indolent a boy he had walked her all the way back from Stratford to Fulham. It could be argued that no other course was open to him to get her there, for he would not have had the courage to tackle the train if he had thought of it; yet it remained for him an extraordinary feat of energy and devotion. There was no question now, it seemed, of considering the Winders' feelings and returning her to them; apart from the fact that Tom was dying of cancer, she had taken to standing on her hind legs against the fence at the bottom of the yard, barking at the trains that passed over the embankment and the neighbors had complained. What I had been expecting of her, if I had been expecting anything, I did not know; but she seemed not at all changed. She had been with Johnny for a week, and although he tried to make light of the problems she presented he admitted they existed and that, in spite of everything that had been said to him about her, he had not realized what she was like. But he had the future all mapped out; when he started work on the following Monday he was going to get up half an hour early to give her a walk first; if his job lay close at hand he'd pop home for dinner and nip her out again then; and in the evenings, when he'd had his tea and cleaned himself up, he'd take her for a good hour's run. Her food was to be "the same as we 'as ourselves," and he was going to get busy at once about finding her a mate. . . .

But when the happy afternoon drew to its close and he put on his coat to go, she did not follow him. Standing between us in the passageway she watched him take down the lead from the rack.

"Come on, old girl," said he, but she did not move, and as soon as this happened I knew that I had known that it would happen, that it had all been decided long ago. With her ears flattened back upon her dark neck, and in a curious crouching attitude, a kind of turntail attitude, yet obstinate too, for her front legs were already braced against any attempt that might be made to drag her forth, she gazed up at him with the unflinching look of a wild beast. He stared at her in surprise.

"Come along, old lady," he said gently, but the only stir she made was to glance swiftly back at me; then she fixed her eyes watchfully on him again. I made no move either; the contest was none of mine, it lay between him and her; but as I leaned up against the jamb of the door I felt that I was not witnessing anything that was happening now, but remembering something that had been enacted in a dream. He took a step towards her; she at once turned and went back past me into my sitting-room.

"Well, would you believe it?" he said, and made to follow her. But I put my arms around him and, halting him on the threshold, drew him towards me.

"Let her stay with me for the weekend, Johnny. It's our due."

"Looks as if I'll 'ave to," said he with a grimace. And

"Would you believe it?" he repeated, though more to himself than to me, and made again to go in after her.

"No!" I said.

"That's all right, Frank," he replied quietly. "I just want to say good-bye to 'er."

I did not enter with him, but I saw what passed between them. Evie was entrenched in the chair, her chin resting on the rampart of the arm, her alert gaze watching the door; when Johnny appeared, her tail began to thump the seat and she looked up at him with a sweet, humble look.

"You faithless woman!" he said reproachfully, and sitting on the arm beside her he fondled her for some time in an abstracted way. Then taking her head between his palms he bent down and kissed her. She licked his hand. She loved him, I could see; but when he came out she remained where she was. Ah yes, I felt sorry for him; I felt for him the pang I saw he felt for himself; he must have known at that moment that he had lost his dog as he had lost his son, but love him too as I did, there was nothing now that I could do about that. Even if I had forced her out—and I knew I could not expel her from my life a second time—he had seen her make her choice, and since there was no doubt that, in his way, he did think the world of her, she hardly could be and, I fear, never was the same to him again. Yes, I saw all that, though not so clearly as, alas, I saw it later, for I saw something else besides, I saw that she loved us both and that, whichever image lay uppermost, we were closely connected in her heart as we had lately been connected in her eyes; like a camera, like a casket, she contained us together, clasped in each other's arms; she was a stronger, a living bond between us.

The prompt return of borrowed dogs to their owners—it was another of the lessons I had lately learnt; I took Evie back to Johnny on the Monday morning and, as though nothing had happened to ruffle it, the future life he had planned for her was put into practice. But I visited them frequently thereafter, and soon things began to turn out as I had foreseen, and a number of things turned out that I might have foreseen if I had studied the signs more diligently. The energetic timetable he had set himself under my critical eye was short-lived, as I knew it would be, partly through his own laziness, partly through one of those extra factors I had not foreseen: Megan became jealous of the dog. Johnny's work did not lie close at hand as he had hoped, and was it likely, when he returned in the evening after being away all day, that she would tamely submit to him going off again for an hour to take Evie for a walk? Besides what else might he not get up to, idling about among other idlers in the Fulham Rec.? Rows started.

"The dog's all you think of," she would say. "You think more of her than you do of me and the children."

"She 'as to 'ave a piss, don't she?" Johnny would retort in a voice of rage, and the flat would resound with argument and recrimination.

But beneath it all, I noticed as time wore on, undercurrents of chaff were discernible. Yell at her as he did, red in the face with pumped-up indignation, Johnny was not wholly unsuited by Megan's objections. His tea, in any case, had always come first and, after his day's work, he was, of course, much in need of it; but Evie had not left the house since eight o'clock in the morning, for no one could hold her but he, and owing to the violent impetuosity of her behavior, which both endangered her life and frightened people in the street, she could not simply be let out like a cat; there was no back yard for her here as there had been at Millie's, and now it was six in the evening. Indeed, I was accustoming myself to seeing other people's points of view and was therefore able to perceive Johnny's when I dropped in around that hour, yet I could not myself, however tired and thirsty I might be, have sat down to my tea in such circumstances before taking the animal out, if only for five minutes, first. But in Johnny's philosophy, it seemed, Evie's bladder and bowels must wait until he was ready for them to open. And since she herself was remarkably obliging at holding everything up, he spent, as time passed, longer and longer over his tea. Megan noticed this too, and quickly took its satisfactory measure. When she wished to be particularly aggravating she would draw attention to it:

"Aren't you going to take the dog out! I thought she had to have a piss?"

"Give us a chance!" Johnny would exclaim, half-annoyed, half-amused. "Can't I swaller me tea first?"

It was I who, calling for her at odd times, mostly took her out at last, on those long, countrified walks she loved, and if Johnny was there to observe the way she flew out of his house with me and related it to her behavior to him in mine, he did not allude to it. It was I too who, in order to save her digestion from Megan's abominable fries, procured her meat, standing for hours, sometimes in the rain and later in the cold, in those immense queues of frantic animal lovers which, at that period, were one of the sights of London. I did not mind. Nothing that I did for Johnny's dog seemed too much trouble. Yet it was, from my own point of view, a far from satisfactory state of affairs, and in the conflict which, I had always known, would break out again between Megan and myself, of the approach of which, indeed, there were already premonitory signs (whether the new child was ever actually christened "Frank", or christened at all, I never ascertained, but although Johnny began calling him "Frankie", Megan dubbed him "David" and that became his name), I too was learning the wisdom of the serpent. While Johnny continued to house his dog I seldom saw him unless I called; since there was scarcely time for her, there was clearly less for me; but if she lived with me—and I was now borrowing her again for single nights and for weekends—then I foresaw that I could get him too. And apart from the many claims I already had to keep her, I was, I perceived, the true master of a situation in which his interests were deeply involved: I was in a far better position than he to breed from her. This was a trump card that could hardly fail to impress not only Johnny but Megan. If Evie was to be the goldmine of expensive pedigree puppies, which, it was increasingly plain, was a project that occupied the forefront of Johnny's mind, how was the mating to be arranged? Fees for the hiring of a stud dog were far beyond his means, and what likelihood was there of a boy in his circumstances and neighborhood happening upon someone who owned a suitably blue-blooded sire and was willing to lend him for nothing? Renouncing, therefore, all claims to past promises, such as that holiday with him, of which, I now guessed, he would be grateful not to be reminded, I made him a proposition. Evie should live with me so that I could look after her more easily; but since I could not cope with her during the week, I should leave her every morning at his place, calling for her on my return from work. If he wanted her at any time to stay with him, he could always have her and for as long as he wished. Finally, I would mate her for him, undertaking all the expense, and the proceeds of the litters should belong wholly to him. He agreed, as I knew he would; after all that I had done for her, and for him, it would have been difficult for him to refuse; what difficulty there was lay in telling, from the quiet "Okay, Frank" with which he let me have my way, what his true feelings were.

We jogged along like this for nearly a year, and it gave me, as I had calculated, the best of both possible worlds; it gave me Johnny's dog and it often gave me Johnny. It was, indeed, while it lasted, the happiest time of my life. Every morning that I had to go to work I walked her over to his flat and parked her there; every afternoon or evening I called for her and walked her back. His keys were left, by arrangement, in a window-box by the door, so that I might let myself in without disturbing Megan. and I would take Evie into the front room and shut her in. She fell in with this routine at once as though she perfectly understood—indeed, it was immensely touching the way she fell in with everything—and made no attempt to follow me when I left. But as she lay down obe-

diently upon the bedding of old coats that Johnny had
spread for her comfort, she fixed on me always, when I
bent to kiss her, so wistful a look, which said as plain as
words "You *will* come back, won't you?", that I never felt
easy in my mind until I found her again. Johnny himself
I seldom saw on these occasions; as seldom did he see his
dog; and all this was as I wished, for it was in my own flat
that I wanted him to meet us and I was always inventing
reasons to get him there. Not that he should need per-
suasions, I thought, only such business excuses as would
enable him to extricate himself with as little dispute
as possible from the jealous possessiveness of Megan,
for how could he resist the prospect of the welcome
that awaited him, not from me—I knew he could resist that—but from Evie? After me he was, and remained,
her favorite man, the only other person that she loved.
She had perceived instantly the truth about him, that,
as Millie had once angrily declared, he was a gentle,
tender-hearted boy, and that he thought the world of
her. She never barked at his approach, as she barked at
the approach of everyone else; she knew unerringly his
step upon the stair, even his odor in the downstairs hall-
way if he had lately passed through ahead of us, and
her snuffling murmurs of excitement communicated the
joyful news to me. And then, when she found him, how
she greeted him, whimpering and sighing in her delight,

licking and licking his handsome face! It was, I always thought as I watched, with a passionate participation, these passionate demonstrations of her love, a proof both of his tenderness towards her and of the essential sweetness of his nature that he never turned his face aside. Over his beautiful lips and eyes, into his nostrils, the dog's tongue would go, as though she could not lick him enough, as though there were something delicious in the taste of his flesh, and he never drew back or turned his face away, but let her lick her fill. And yet this love she lavished upon him, did it not contain the seeds of sorrow? He was second best, he knew it and that he never could be more to her than that, and the more therefore she laid it on, this one-man dog of his to whom he was not the one man, the more he must have felt what he had lost. Indeed, I saw it, for when she had done making love to him he would make love to her. He knew, as though by instinct, exactly where and how to touch her, and as soon as his hand descended she would roll over on her side and open her legs, and his strong yet gentle fingers would move over her stomach, manipulating her nipples and her neat, pretty genital, shaped like the crown of a daffodil, in a way she enjoyed, while he whispered little affectionate obscenities into her ears. "Is this it, gal? Is this what you like?" he would say, and she would sigh and swoon away beneath him. Yet she never followed him; and though sometimes, when we saw him part-way home along the towing-path, he would test her again, out of a lingering curiosity, perhaps a lingering disbelief, by inviting her to go with him, she stayed at my side; but she would look back from time to time at his small receding figure, a sweet thing he never did for us. Yes, she knew he thought the world of her; but possibly, I reflected, she guessed, as I now did, what the world amounted to, and that what he had just done for us was, of all things she wanted, the most she would ever get, and that she could not count even on that.

It was because of all this, I felt sure, that he seldom exercised the right he had to take her from me. I put no hint nor hesitation in his way; on the contrary I sometimes reminded him of his right, for as well as the sense of sorrow I felt for him, I had, in the very gladness I felt for myself, a sense of guilt, that I, and Millie too for that matter, had managed somehow to despoil him of his possessions at a moment when he had been powerless to defend them. His possessions or, less concedable, more outrageous, some part of himself that he did not wish to give, something that his heart was unwilling any longer to submit to ours. At any rate, whatever it was that we had done to him and whatever he felt, whether he knew that, in spite of my reminders, I found it increasingly hard to part with Evie, or whether he himself found it increasingly hard to face the fact that, when she was with him and love him as she did, she was always listening for me, he did not ask for her much. And so it passed, this strange, sad, pretty time in which she lived between us and held us reticently together; for came a day when we had a conversation which shed over the whole past a bleak and bitter light. He began it.

"I'm not saying you're wrong about all this, Frank. I'm not saying that. But there's two ways of looking at it."

"Oh, Johnny," I said, "I'm sure there are. But looking at what?"

"Well, it's like this. If I 'adn't got nicked screwin' and Evie 'ad lived with me as my dog, she'd 'ave 'ad a different life from what she's 'ad with you, if you see what I mean; but that's not to say she wouldn't 'ave been just as well off."

"I suppose that would depend upon the kind of life you gave her."

"No, it wouldn't. Not to my way of thinking. That's what I mean. Whatever it was, she'd 'ave got used to it and been just as well off."

I turned this over in my mind.

"As happy?"

"Yes, as 'appy. What you've never 'ad you never miss. If I'd 'ad 'er all along, I'd 'ave brought 'er up me own way. I'd 'ave took 'er out first thing in the morning for 'er piddles, then she'd 'ave 'ad it until I come in for me tea. After that I'd 'ave took 'er up to the pub and she'd 'ave sat there quiet beside me while I 'ad a few pints and a game of darts. Then she'd 'ave walked 'ome be'ind me afterwards. Weekends I'd 'ave took 'er farther."

Evie had now developed talents; she had become a skillful rabbiter, pelting a daily fifteen miles in Richmond Park. I was about to say this when I saw that it was, of course, the very thing he meant. The conversation had begun to worry me. I said lightly:

"Ah, Johnny, none of your poor dogs gets all he wants from you, and we love you just the same."

But he was not to be deflected. It was as though he was determined to make nonsense of the past.

"It's all what you're used to, see? Of course it wouldn't do now, because she's 'ad a different way of life and she'd miss it. But if she'd 'ad my way instead, she'd 'ave been just as 'appy, for she wouldn't 'ave known no better."

Perhaps it was true. I did not want to look. I was happy again myself—and I knew that my happiness was vulnerable. What he was inviting me to look at was the world he thought of his creatures, and it was his world, not ours. Into it we were required to fit, patient and undemanding, awaiting our sops, the walk, the letter, the visit, the descending hand. Evie herself had managed to escape from it. As for me, I did not want to look. I said, vaguely teasing:

"Then you do think mine better?"

"No, I wouldn't even say that. I didn't mean it that way. What I mean is, 'ow many dogs, town dogs, gets as much exercise as Evie gets? Not one in a 'undred. Not one in a thousand. Now do they? Lots of them never do no more than sit about outside the shops and 'ouses where they belong, yet you can't say they're un'appy, for they don't know nothing else, and you can't say they're un'ealthy, for they grows old like any other dog what's 'ad a different life. . . ."

Yes, it was true, and it had all been useless. I saw it now and how pitiful it was. It had been a mistake from beginning to end, the total struggle, all that love and labor, passion and despair; it had all been hopeless and unavailing; I had lost the fight for him before ever it had begun.

"Do you see what I mean?" he asked.

"Oh yes, Johnny. That I should never have interfered."

"Now, now, I didn't mean nothing like that. What I meant was——"

"That everything was perfectly all right."

"I'm not blaming you, mind. It was me own fault, and you done your best, I know. All I'm saying is——"

"That I've spoiled your life."

Then the rot set in. The pleasant precarious situation came to an end. Evie hastened it, for in two successive heats the matings she submitted to did not take and she began to be suspected, in the phrase of a breeder, of being "a barren bitch." With the failure of the prospective goldmine the party started to break up. Appointments with Johnny were less easily made, more frequently forgotten or defeated; yet at the same time he began to put in claims for her oftener than he had done before.... Then he failed an engagement that included her. He had taken her for a few days and was to have brought her along to visit me on a certain evening. He neither came nor phoned. That shattered me. If I could get on now without him or without her, a future that contained neither was one I could not enter. I hurried to Fulham. The house was in darkness, the keys were not in their place, no one came to my rattling. And recollecting that other occasion when I had drummed upon the empty house, a cold terror seized me that this was what I was destined to do, that this was my inescapable fate for ever and ever. What could have happened? Where could they be? I hastened over to the pub he frequented and searched it in vain. Then I remembered another, smaller pub he sometimes used, and there he was, alone, standing in the public bar with a pint of beer in front of him.

"Evie?" I said.

"She's indoors. She's okay. 'Ave a drink."

Now, my agitation stilled, I noticed him, and saw that it was the same old story. Always, before coming out of an evening, he smartened himself up, but he was wearing his working clothes; his thick dark curly hair, over the arrangement of which he normally took great pains, was unbrushed; the side of his face was badly scratched. I had seen it many times before and did not have to ask questions. I knew that after their row, over me of course, Megan had rushed off in a rage to spend the evening with her friends, but that the jealousy that had shot her off would soon swing her back to search for him; I knew that he would again refer to her as a "bloody cow," and that this pub, which he had selected for its less embarrassing publicity, was as far from her as he would ever get; I knew that he would stay here dumbly pouring pints into himself and urinating them out until she came and found him; I knew that the wrangle would be resumed, by her and on a more perfunctory note to cloak the starkness of her triumph, that she would shame him into buying her a drink by demanding it in a voice loud enough to be overheard, that he would stalk sullenly home beside her and copulate with her before dawn, and that peace would then be restored—until he attempted to assert himself again; and I knew that he was pleased to see me and that

I was, and always had been, powerless to help him. If he had really needed me he would have come to me in spite of her.

"Drink up!" said he.

How boyish he looked with his hair in a muddle—as he used to look, once upon a time.

"Johnny," I said, in sudden desperation, "let's get away from here! Come with me! Do what you promised to do! You can stay the night or as long as you like. We'll take Evie too! The three of us together! How wonderful it will be! Come! Do come!"

"Ah-h, I'm not in the mood. Drink up!"

I was no use to him. I stood him a drink. Then I asked:

"May I take Evie back with me?"

"I've only 'ad 'er a coupler days. You can fetch 'er Monday."

"All right. I'll be getting along then."

"What d'you want to go for? It's early."

"Megan will be here at any moment."

"Ah, sod 'er!"

I turned towards him.

"Johnny, if you don't want me, go back to Evie! She'd give you such a welcome! Go now and take her for a nice long walk! How happy you would make her!"

"She's all right. I'll take 'er round before I turn in."

I said gently: "But that's routine. Give her something

special tonight, a surprise, a present. She does love you
so much."

"Ah-h, I feel like getting pissed."

"Then you won't be able to take her afterwards," I said
with a smile.

"I can always keep me feet."

We were no use to him, either of us. He thought the
world of us both, and we were no use to him at all. She
lonely in his kitchen, I lonely in my flat, and neither of us
any use to him, lonely in his pub. That was what I saw,
standing beside him in the sad little place; and it was
true. A few days later he remarked, with a laugh, that
someone was wanting to buy her.

"Johnny!" I cried. "Give her to me! She belongs to
me!"

I tried to meet his eyes, but they would not meet mine.

"I can't do that," he muttered, gnawing his nails.

Now I could not look at him either as I said:

"Well, if you sell her, you can sell her to no one
but me."

"Who said I meant to sell her?" he replied irritably.

Nothing more was said just then, but he had frightened me over a wide area; by the time the subject came
up again, as I feared it would, I had decided upon my
answer. Evie had already been valued, at his request, by a
breeder we had visited together, who had hazarded the

rough figure of "about thirty or forty pounds." This was in her gold-mine period when we were seeking a husband for her; her value now could be nothing like that. But when a little later Johnny told me that some pub acquaintance of his was "absolutely crazing" him to sell her and had even called round to ask him to name a price, I could risk it no longer. What his intentions really were I did not know, but they must now be put to the fatal test. I said:

"If you ever decide to sell her, Johnny, it must be to me, and I will give you forty pounds for her any day."

He did not reply. But the next day—alas, poor Johnny, I knew that if it happened at all it would be the next day, it was what I both dreaded and desired—he came over unannounced.

"Did you mean what you said about the forty quid?"

"Of course."

"Give it me," said he roughly.

In this way Evie became my dog. But since I was still in the same predicament of being unable to keep her single-handed, I stipulated, as part of the bargain, that the old arrangement should continue until I could make other plans. It had never been satisfactory and for Evie herself I had long regarded it as actually bad; she was a creature much in need of the stabilizing influence of a settled life and a home of her own where she could function confidently in her canine way, and the divided life she had been leading, in which she never could feel sure to whom she belonged, must be very frustrating for her: but in any case the affair was doomed. Now that the dog had passed, I, in Megan's scheme of things, could pass also; an outward show of politeness was maintained, but behind it she was working my total destruction. So everything went back to what it had been before; Johnny scarcely ever came to see me; if I wrote to him my letters were intercepted and suppressed; the keys began to be forgotten, so that either I could not put the dog in or could not get her out, and sometimes spent an agitated hour or more hanging about their street with little Rita for unhelpful company. Megan was not clever enough to see that she was waging war against an adversary who had already capitulated. Her interferences in my life with Johnny no longer aroused in me the black and murderous passions they had once aroused; it was only when she started to withhold the keys that I perceived that my connection with them both was at an end. On one of my last rare meetings with Johnny, when Evie had done lavishing upon him her unfailing, her wonderful, greeting, he remarked as he stroked her glowing head:

"You 'ad the best of the bargain."

I knew, of course, to what bargain he referred; but when I looked across her body into the eyes that had once affected me so deeply and now affected me no more, and nodded, it was not of that bargain that I was thinking.

And that, it might be thought, is the end of the story; but of course it was only the beginning. A new character, even, has to be introduced, though luckily for the dramatic unities a not entirely fresh one, for she has already played a small peripheral part.

During the two years whose events this history has attempted to relate, the fortunes of my country cousin suffered a serious reverse. It was a reverse I might have prevented if I had not been too distracted to give her that advice over her financial affairs which she had requested at the time of Miss Sweeting. In the result she speculated unwisely and lost a considerable part of her income. As her nearest relative she had always looked to me for help. Nearest and dearest: the most salient thing about my cousin Margaret was that she thought the world of me. It had, indeed, long been her wish to enter and manage my life; it had long been my concern to fend her off. The bachelor is often considered fair game to those relations, particularly the female part of them, whose own lives have become empty or straitened: poor, helpless fellow, the formula runs, he needs a woman's care.

And now the trouble was that I did need care, though

not for myself. The connection was all too patent: since the responsibility for assisting my cousin had fallen on me, the economic temptation presented itself of getting some return for my money by employing her to mind my dog. It was, in the event, a temptation I would have been wise to resist and, sensing the dangers, I did not succumb to it at once. I began by advertising for a boy. Evie was already an object of awed admiration to the local children; might not a steady one be found who would be glad to earn a little pocket money by helping me with her? But although a stream of willing urchins called, I could not bring myself to entrust her to any of them—and was therefore able to add another point of view, poor Millie's, to those I was collecting. In the end I took on my cousin in the capacity of kennel-maid and, since I could not afford her a separate establishment, housed her in my flat.

This entailed considerable sacrifice on my part. My flat was small. It comprised virtually only two rooms, my bedroom and my sitting-room, for the lobby that separated them and which I used as a dining-room was scarcely more than an extension of the passage. In order to fit my cousin in, therefore, I had to relinquish one of these rooms. I bestowed upon her my bedroom, retreating myself into my sitting-room which contained a small divan bed and thenceforward became my bed-sitting-room. Evie, of course retreated with me; but it was at once apparent that these innovations, which I myself was prepared to endure entirely for her sake, did not please her.

It would be no overstatement to declare that from the moment Evie achieved her ambition, which was to get me to herself in a home of her own, her true character was instantly revealed. There had been indications of it before, but I had misread them. Her persistent hostility to strangers may well have been compounded of various emotions, nervousness, suspicion, and a desire to protect me; but all these, I now realized, were overridden by something infinitely stronger, an intense, possessive jealousy.

Directly Margaret arrived, Evie laid down the law. The law was simple and, in my judgment, reasonable; she was prepared, since it appeared to be my wish, to put up with my cousin and allow her about the flat—with one proviso: our room, hers and mine, whenever I was at home, was strictly private. This suited me well, I value solitude and, suspecting that my cousin did not, had already apprehended that I might have to struggle to preserve what little remained to me. This prospect made me rather uneasy, for, to speak the truth, I was nervous of Margaret. She was one of those people whose virtues (and she was far from being without them) are apparent only when they are getting their own way; opposed there was something cold and ruthless about her. And I was wary of her for another reason, for the very quality in her which I have already mentioned, that she thought the world of me. I did not therefore altogether relish providing that display of firmness which, I foresaw, might be required before a *modus vivendi* was reached. Evie provided it for me.

She would not permit my cousin to set foot in my room. More, with a female instinct for female strategem, she would not permit any of those first moves—that thin edge of the wedge—which might lead to this result. She challenged my cousin's right to knock upon the door, even to approach it, even to call to me through it. All these maneuvers were instantly greeted with a volley of violent and hysterical barking. Her mind, indeed, when I was at home, was entirely occupied with this anxiety, this menace—as she appeared to regard it—to her marital rights. It was extraordinary, it was fascinating, to watch her. As soon as I shut us both in, she would take up an invariable position on the bed which, standing as it did against the wall by the door, gave her a strategic command over the latter. Arranging herself in a vigilant attitude upon the end nearest the door and facing it, she would lie, or rather crouch, there listening. I would look up from my book and see her, absolutely still, wonderfully beautiful, her long nose pointing down to the bottom of the door, her head tilted, her great ears cocked forward, attentively following my cousin's movements outside. If she detected in these, to me inaudible, sounds what seemed to her the smallest tendency to vacillate, to veer, she would instantly utter a sharp warning bark and, raising her head, stare fixedly at the ceiling. This curious motion puzzled me for a time; then I perceived the reason for it. The door was draped inside by a long curtain that bulged out over a miscellany of garments which were hanging beneath it, and Evie could not therefore see the door itself or the handle. Moreover, a constant slight draught kept the curtain always stirring a little. Consequently it was difficult for her to tell, by looking at it, whether the door itself was moving; but this she could ascertain by studying the ceiling, upon which, when the door opened, a widening arc of light was instantly cast from the dining-room outside. The moment she saw this, for which she was perpetually waiting, she would launch herself off the bed in a passion of vocal rage and, planting herself on the threshold, her tail lashing from side to side, bar my cousin's entry.

All this, as I have said, suited me nicely. But it did not suit my cousin. Having gained, upon any terms, the object of her desire, a foothold in my flat, she planned, as I feared she would, to become mistress of it, and it was deeply mortifying for her to find another, self-constituted, mistress already installed, and one, moreover, of a character as determined as her own. It was not long, therefore, before she developed a point of view, which of course I saw: even if the discernment of points of view had not now become a speciality of mine I could hardly have failed to notice hers, I heard it so often. Evie never behaved like this in my absence; she was quiet, docile, amenable; she accepted everything without demur and did not even oppose my cousin's entry into the sacred but now deserted chamber. It was therefore disgusting, it was the basest ingratitude, to be turned on by the dog—"After all I've done for her!"—the moment I came back; and it was all my fault, I spoiled Evie, I let her do anything she liked, I ought to pet her less and punish her more, I ought (this, I sadly noted, was one of my cousin's favorite words) not to allow her to sleep in my room, I was turning her into a beastly dog, jealous and treacherous. . . .

Let there be no doubt of it, I was extremely grateful to my cousin. She was kind to Evie, and the services she rendered me, not only by setting me free for my work and holidays but by setting me free with an easy mind, could not, I gladly admit, have been better performed by anyone else. She was, in short, what I knew she would be, a perfectly reliable kennel-maid; and that, after all, was the capacity in which I had engaged her. But it was not the capacity in which she saw herself. All her complaints about Evie were entirely, were delightfully, true; the animal was *not* the same in my absence; but they were not the truth. The truth was that, like Megan, she was jealous of the dog. She could not bear that Evie should have privileges denied to her. She could not bear to be excluded by her. The thought of the animal inside my room and herself outside gnawed at her vitals. The closed door that shut her out stood always before her, a frustration, a persecution, an affront, and a challenge. She was forever plotting to get into the room simply because she knew she was not welcome in it; and Evie was forever plotting to keep her out. It was the strangest, the most prodigious, thing I ever saw, this duel that was fought between my cousin and my dog. I would leave the room for some purpose and Evie who went with me everywhere, would follow at my heels. This provided my cousin with the opportunity for which she lay ceaselessly in wait, her need to enter the room having become so obsessive that merely to slip into it, this citadel of my love, even at such an apparently undefended moment, seemed to her a compensation and a score. Upon some small pre-text or other, therefore— to empty an ashtray, to remove a used cup, duties for which she had not been engaged but which she liked to regard as within her scope—she would make her little housewifely dart. But Evie's jealousy appeared to have equipped her with human faculties and a cunning equal to her adversary's; she sensed my cousin's intentions almost before they entered the realm of action. With lowered head and a movement of quite uncanny stealth she would turn and glide rapidly back along the passage wall, thrust herself roughly past my cousin's legs, nipping at her feet as she went, so that my cousin yelped with pain, and intercept her on the threshhold.

Then my cousin changed her tactics. She tried to win the dog away from me with love. And now, alas for the lessons of life, alas for human faith, my heart misgave me. Had I prepared my own undoing? I had wanted Evie happy in my absences, and they were becoming longer and more frequent; my cousin was feeding her daily and doing for her all the things I used to do myself; she was seeing far more of her than I. Indeed, it was all as I had desired and planned; excepting that I did not want to lose my dog. When I thought of losing her I trembled with the kind of internal cold that seems the presage of death. I loved her; I wished her forever happy; but I could not bear to lose her. I could not bear even to share her. She was my true love and I wanted her all to myself. I was afflicted, in short, by the same fear that had haunted poor Johnny in his prison, the fear that he might lose his second Evie as he had lost his first. One night she was missing from my room. I woke suddenly in the dark early hours; the air was strangely cold; the chair was empty. Where could she be?

I got up and hunted the flat; she was nowhere to be found. My cousin's door was closed; she was inside my cousin's room; she had chosen my cousin. I returned to my bed and lay down on it in the darkness. "This is the end," I thought. "She loves my cousin more than me. I can never care for her again. I am alone in the cold, cruel world." Then in the distance I heard, like the sorrow of a ghost, the faint whistling sigh she made through her nose when she was grieving. Creeping back to my cousin's door I gently turned the handle. Evie at once emerged and reentered my room. She had not been on my cousin's bed, she had been lying by the door; my cousin had enticed and shut her in against her will. I knew then that she was my dog for ever and ever, and I fell asleep with the peacefulness of a child.

But peace for my poor cousin there was none. As my confidence increased, so did her resentment. Unable to corrupt the animal with love, she pitted herself once more against her, trying her strength by provoking the very situation she could neither brook nor ignore. She was always calling out to me through the closed door, or rapping upon it, or even opening it and entering the forbidden chamber. The arc upon the ceiling would widen and, with the ferocity of a tigress, Evie would launch herself off the bed. It was pandemonium. It was worse, it was murder. But my cousin was not to be baulked. She was determined to enter the room. She was prepared, if necessary, to die in the attempt. With an expression of disdain on her pale stony face she would stand there in the doorway, while Evie's shrieking jaws snapped at her dangling, motionless hands. Resignedly awaiting the opportunity to make herself heard and without so much as a glance at the maddened dog, she would stand there, or even move further forward, pushing against the animal's snarling mouth, in her own eyes a martyr, in mine an avenging fury. For I knew she had nothing to say, nothing that could not wait; she had another end in view; she desired me to punish my dog. To force this issue she was gambling now with her highest card, her very life; I fancy she never guessed how thoughtfully I considered it. But tremendous courage and resolution are required to watch someone actually torn to pieces before one's eyes without intervening. As will already have been perceived from these confessions, I do not possess such courage and resolution. Upon this, no doubt, my cousin banked. She knew that I would intervene and the form the intervention would take; between seeing her destroyed and striking my dog I had no other alternative. Words were ineffectual, if heard; I would have to drive Evie off with blows. That was what my cousin willed and that was what I did. Yes, I often struck my faithful dog for her inestimable faithfulness, for performing the duty of guarding my solitude which I wished her to perform, while the cold figure of my cousin stood silently by willing this revenge and viewing my corrections with a jealous inquisitorial eye to see that they were met. And every curse that I gave the sweet creature, every blow that I laid upon her body, was a lie—and from any educative point of view happily a useless one, for Evie's jealousy was as indestructible as my cousin's, and the whole scene would be re-enacted, in precisely the same way, the next time my cousin tried it on, even if it were only a few minutes later.

I hardly remember for how long these two formidable females, the hairy and the hairless one, struggled for my possession. It was certainly more than a year. Naturally it was rather distracting; it was also extremely instructive. I perceived that the intolerable situation from which I had escaped in Johnny's house was being reproduced in my own, though with a difference. The difference, of course, and it was an undeniable improvement, was that I was now the subject instead of the object of jealousy. Poor Margaret was the latter, and it did not fail to secure for her both my sympathy for her sufferings and my respect for her valor to note that she occupied the odious position I had occupied before. Nor did I omit to pay the final tribute: I saw Megan's point of view. The treacherous little Welsh runt of a couple of years

ago, how could I help now but regard her as a female of
heroic stature, as ruthless, uncompromising and incor-
ruptible as Evie? Both were prepared to fight tooth and
nail and to the finish to secure to themselves, and to
themselves alone, the love of their chosen male. And
both of them won. After a time my cousin retired, broken
in health, crushed in spirit, leaving Evie in undisputed
possession of my life.

Since then she has set herself to keep everyone else
out of it. None of the succession of visiting helps I engaged to supply my cousin's place stayed longer than a
few days; even the sparrows and pigeons that try to perch
on my verandah are instantly put to flight; no fly enters
and survives; she would know if I stroked another animal
on my way home for she smells me all over directly I
return and I should suffer from remorse if I hurt her feelings; she cannot actually read my correspondence, but
she seizes it all as it falls through the letter-box and
tears it to shreds. Advancing age has only intensified her
jealousy. I have lost all my old friends, they fear her and
look at me with pity or contempt. We live entirely alone.
Unless with her I can never go away. I can scarcely call
my soul my own. Not that I am complaining, oh no; yet
sometimes as we sit and my mind wanders back to
the past, to my youthful ambitions and the freedom
and independence I used to enjoy, I wonder what in the

world has happened to me and how it all came about. . . .
But that leads me into deep waters, too deep for fathoming; it leads me into the darkness of my own mind.